YOU'RE IN THE JUNIORS NOW

about the author

Margaret Joy is the author of a number of books for younger children. She has worked as a school teacher, and this provided the setting for many of her books. Her husband is head of a school for deaf children. They have four children, now grown up. They live in Wales.

YOU'RE IN THE JUNIORS NOW

Margaret Joy

Illustrated by Jo Burroughes

faber and faber
LONDON · BOSTON

First published in Great Britain in 1988
by Faber and Faber Limited
3 Queen Square London WC1N 3AU
This paperback edition first published in 1991

Printed in England by Clays Ltd, St Ives plc

Margaret Joy is hereby identified as the author
of this work in accordance with Section 77 of
the Copyright, Designs and Patents Act 1988

A CIP record for this book is available from the
British Library

ISBN 0-571-16461-7

4 6 8 10 9 7 5 3

CONTENTS

1

SEPTEMBER

New Term, New Teacher

'You must have a hair-cut,' said Mum, eyeing Foxy's sprouting ginger hair. 'Your head looks like a coconut.'

'I like it like this,' scowled Foxy.

'And it's time you had some new winter shoes,' said Dad. 'Those red and black trainers are in a dreadful state.'

'I like my trainers,' said Foxy. 'They're comfortable. What's all the fuss about?'

'Haven't you looked at the calendar?' asked Mum. 'Have you forgotten what next Monday is?'

Foxy looked at her, then at his Dad. Gran shook her head sorrowfully.

' "Shades of the prison-house begin to close upon the growing boy," ' she said with relish.

'Oh, you and your poetry, Mother,' said Mum. 'Don't put him off.'

She turned to Foxy. 'She means that Monday's

the first day of the school term.'

Foxy felt as though a heavy stone had dropped on to the floor of his stomach. He remembered Mrs Griffiths saying goodbye to them at the end of last term; she had looked really sad. Then she had given each of them a bar of chocolate for a goodbye present.

'When you come back to school in September, you'll all be rough, tough juniors,' she said. 'But you'll enjoy being with Mr Tucker; he's full of surprises. And don't forget – his bark is worse than his bite.'

Foxy had seen Mr Tucker striding along the corridor, but no one had ever heard him barking – and surely teachers weren't allowed to bite children – were they? ... Foxy wished he was going back to nice Mrs Griffiths. She always gave out sweets when it was somebody's birthday, and she let them choose what activities they wanted on Friday afternoons.

'Whose class will you be in now?' asked Gran.

Foxy didn't want to have to say Mr Tucker's name out loud. He scowled.

'Oh . . . er 'm not really sure,' he said.

On Monday morning he stood miserably on the doorstep. He was washed and brushed and was wearing a new pullover, new socks and heavy new lace-ups.

2

'"Creeping like snail unwillingly to school,"' said Gran, giving him a quick kiss.

'Oh, leave him alone, Mother,' said Mum. 'He'll be all right.'

Betsy stood on the doorstep in her dungarees and waved too. Then she realized that Foxy was going off somewhere interesting without her, and she started to scream.

'Me, too; me, too!' she yelled, and stamped her feet up and down on the step. Foxy turned back, his face brightening.

3

'Shall I stay and make her better?' he offered.

Then he saw the firm expression on his Mum's face and realized that there was nothing for it: he had to go. He set off slowly along the street.

When he reached his new classroom, most of his friends were already there. The walls were bare and there was a strong smell of disinfectant. The room seemed cold; Foxy shivered. Then he spotted Imran's dark hair and went over to him.

'Hey – look at your shoes,' said Imran. 'They new?'

Foxy nodded glumly; they were already beginning to rub his heels. He asked,

'Your jeans new, too?'

'Yeah,' said Imran. 'It's like walking in cardboard.'

They stood together in silence, leaning against the wall. Other people were looking rather apprehensive, too. Kevin Wilson stationed himself on guard, peering through a crack in the door.

'Oh, dear,' whispered Lucy. 'I don't think I want a man teacher.'

Loud footsteps echoed down the corridor, coming nearer.

'It's him,' hissed Kevin.

They all scattered and flung themselves towards the nearest chairs. Foxy and Imran made for the same one.

4

'Geddoff,' hissed Foxy. 'I'm on this one.'

'No, you're not, I was on it first,' said Imran.

'It's mine – geddoff,' glared Foxy.

'It's mine!' insisted Imran.

They each sat, half on, half off the chair, furiously pushing shoulder to shoulder with all their strength.

'Gett*off*,' cried Foxy, kicking at Imran's legs.

'It's *mine*,' yelled Imran, digging a bony elbow into Foxy's ribs.

The rest of the class were frozen in their seats. There was a long and horrible silence. Foxy and Imran suddenly realized that Mr Tucker was standing in the doorway – waiting. They faltered to their feet very sheepishly.

'YOU – go there,' barked Mr Tucker to Foxy, pointing at another chair. 'And YOU – there,' he pointed at Imran and then to another chair across the room.

The two boys slunk to their places and sat down. Mr Tucker looked long and hard at Imran, then at Foxy, then at the rest of the class. The children hardly dared to breathe; they could have heard a pin drop.

'I will *not* have fighting in my class!' thundered Mr Tucker suddenly, and everybody jumped.

There was another long pause. Mr Tucker surveyed his new class. They took quick glances at him without meeting his eyes: dark hair, dark beard, green jacket. How on earth would they get on together for three whole terms? At last Mr Tucker broke the silence.

'You're in the Juniors now, you lot; things are bound to be a little strange at first. But I'm sure you'll soon get used to my way of doing things

. . . In a minute we'll talk about the timetable – there's a lot to fit into each week, what with times for swimming, games and the computer, as well as language and number work and other things. I hope you'll join in some of the lunch-time clubs and after-school activities too. But first of all we'll go quickly through the register, so that I get to know your names.'

CRA-ASSHH! Everyone jumped. Lucy had been nervously fiddling with her pencil tin, and it had fallen off the edge of the table and crashed to the floor. She burst into tears.

Mr Tucker didn't say a word. He took no notice of Lucy. All eyes followed him as he stood up, went to the back of the room and reached down behind a cupboard. Lucy was still sobbing noisily. He lifted up something rather heavy and carried it carefully back to his table. He laid it down and began to stroke it. Everyone stared. Then they began to murmur comments. Lucy hiccuped noisily and wiped her eyes, then she stared too.

'This is Doris,' said Mr Tucker.

Doris was an enormously fat grey rabbit. She lay contentedly twitching her whiskers and looking at the children, while Mr Tucker stroked her smooth fur.

'She lives in a hutch at night,' he said. 'But in

the day-time she prefers to stay in her warm hidey-hole behind the cupboard – I think she likes to be near the radiator.'

It was quiet again for a while, as everyone watched Mr Tucker gently stroking Doris. He turned to Lucy.

'Would you like to come and stroke her?' he asked.

Lucy thought about it, then slowly nodded. She went up to Mr Tucker's table and began to smooth down the fur on Doris's head and long ears.

'Now, while Doris is being looked after,' said Mr Tucker, 'I must tell you all about another visitor we're going to have today. He's called Bill, and he's an old friend of mine. The Headmaster knows he's coming. He's a farmer, and he said he'd be over here at ten o'clock.'

Mr Tucker looked at his watch, then put his head on one side and seemed to be listening.

'Ah, yes, he's spot on time,' he said. 'I can hear him now – I told you he'd be over here at ten o'clock.'

The children could hear a loud noise outside and beyond the classroom. It was growing steadily louder: raka-taka-taka-taka-taka-taka.

Foxy was near the window. He looked upwards.

'There's a helicopter,' he said. 'An orange helicopter . . . it's coming down, it's coming down –
it's coming down *here*!'

'Good,' said Mr Tucker calmly. 'That must be
Bill – he said he'd be dropping in.'

The grass round the edges of the playground
suddenly began to swish to and fro. The noise
was growing louder: raka-taka-taka-taka-*taka*-
TAKA. A shadow hovered across the classroom
windows. Then the helicopter itself came slowly
down into view. It was so close that they could
see the pilot in a blue jacket. And then it had
landed, its rotor blades still whirling.

By now all the children were on their feet,
hardly believing what they were seeing. The
rotor blades began to whirl more slowly. The
pilot opened his door and climbed down. Then,
keeping his head low, he ran across to the outside door. Mr Tucker led him into the classroom.
The two men shook hands.

'Hello, Bill – good of you to drop in.'

'Hi, Chris, good to see you.'

'May I introduce Doris?' said Mr Tucker.

'Hi, Doris,' said Bill.

'And – ?' Mr Tucker looked questioningly at
Lucy.

'Lucy,' she whispered.

'Hi, Lucy,' said Bill.

'And my class,' said Mr Tucker.

'Hi, class,' said Bill.

'They've probably got lots of things they want to ask you about,' said Mr Tucker.

'Oh, yes, sure – they can come outside in a minute and have a closer look at the chopper.'

'Wow! ... Great! ... Triff! ... Brill! ... Ace! ...'

But the pilot wasn't really paying attention. He was looking round the room and grinning.

'Do you know, Chris, this just reminds me of when we were in the Juniors together – it doesn't seem that long ago, does it? Do you remember that time you and I had a good old set-to in the middle of old Sherbet's maths lesson? We were really lamming into one another – you had me by the hair because I'd just kicked your shins for breaking my ruler –'

'No, you had *me* by the hair because you thought I'd copied you in the test –'

'No, no, Chris – you had *me* by the hair –'

'No, Bill, you've got it all wrong –'

'I remember distinctly –'

'You're wrong –'

The two men suddenly realized that they had an audience. The children were listening wide-eyed. Foxy and Imran exchanged embarrassed glances. The pilot began to laugh.

'Don't take any notice of us,' he said to the class. 'It was a long time ago – and we're still friends. Now – who fancies coming outside to have a look at the chopper?'

'Ooh, me! . . . Me, sir . . . Me, please . . . and me . . . and me, and me, and me!'

Everyone in the class was jumping up and down eagerly, dying to get outside and see the helicopter from close quarters. The pilot grinned and turned to Mr Tucker.

'Nice lot of kids you've got here, Chris,' he said. 'Looks like you're in for a good year.'

'Mmm,' growled Mr Tucker into his beard. 'That remains to be seen.'

2

OCTOBER

Hallowe'en

'I'm a Horrifibiter,' said Imran.

'I'm a Fierceychewemup,' said Foxy.

Their eyes glittered dangerously as they stared at each other through the eyeholes in their masks.

'Right, everyone,' called Mr Tucker. 'Clear up every single scrap, please, before you go. I want the paints put away and all this card and poly-styrene picked up. If Mrs Beatty comes in here to clean and finds all this rubbish on the floor, she'll turn me into a toad – it is Hallowe'en, after all.'

'You wouldn't be able to teach us, if you were a toad, would you, sir?' said Kevin.

'Ah, but she might turn me into a tiger instead,' warned Mr Tucker. 'That might make things tricky for you . . . so come on: every scrap cleared up, please.'

Later, Foxy and Imran sauntered along the school road together, wearing their masks. The

Horrifibiter was covered in purple warts, and had fearsome horns and a straggly beard. The Fierceychewemup had pointed shark's teeth and an enormous green nose; its woodshaving hair stuck out all round in springy curls. As the two boys walked along, they enjoyed seeing the effect they had on passers-by. A toddler hid its eyes in its mother's skirt; a baby in a pram bounced up and down, dribbling in disbelief; the policeman at the corner narrowed his eyes and stared back at them; a dog crossed the road to avoid them. But the lollipop lady said:

'Well, hello, Foxy and Imran.'

'How do you know it's us?' asked Foxy in his Fierceychewemup voice.

13

'I recognize you both by your feet,' she said. 'Imran always wears those stripy socks – and I'd know Foxy's red and black trainers anywhere.'

'But I'm a Fierceychewemup,' roared Foxy.

'And I'm a Horrifibiter,' said Imran.

'Very nice, too,' said the lollipop lady. 'And I suppose you'll be out in those masks hallowe'ening tonight?'

'Course,' nodded the two monsters; they liked the idea of padding the streets in disguise.

By six o'clock it was quite dark. A few stars twinkled overhead, and the air smelt of frost. The two boys put on their masks and knocked at Mrs Bell's door. She opened it and stared. The monsters began to chant:

'The sky is blue, the grass is green, have you got a penny for Hallowe'en?'

'Oh, my goodness,' said Mrs Bell. 'What . . . awful creatures. Well, I haven't any pennies for you, but I've just made some gingerbread and it's still warm. Would you like a piece?'

Without waiting for an answer, she went back into the kitchen and brought back two large pieces of gingerbread which she gave to the monsters.

'We used to call Hallowe'en "Mischief Night", when I was young,' she said.

She nodded at them and closed the door. They

walked slowly down the path and stood at the gate. They had to push their masks up over their heads so they could eat the gingerbread.

'We forgot to do Trick or Treat,' said Imran with his mouth full.

'We'll do that next,' said Foxy.

They rang the bell at Mr Porrett's door. He opened it and stood there in his shirtsleeves and slippers.

'Trick or Treat?' growled the Horrifibiter.

'Trick or Treat?' roared the Fierceychewemup.

'Oh, treat, of course,' said Mr Porrett. 'How about treacle toffee?'

He held out a dish he had placed ready by the door, and they each took a large piece.

'Great,' said the Horrifibiter, forgetting to growl.

'Yummy,' said the Fierceychewemup.

They sat on the wall, sucking and chewing, until the toffee was finished. Then they jumped down and crunched their way up Mrs Mundy's drive.

'The sky is blue, the grass is green, have you got a penny for Hallowe'en?'

'Yes,' said Mrs Mundy, 'I thought some Halloweenies might call tonight, so I put some pennies ready. Here you are.'

The two boys held out their hands and she

placed a large brown coin on to each of them.

'Now I don't believe in handing out money for you to buy sweets with to rot your teeth,' she said. 'So I'm giving you Victorian bun pennies. You can't spend them, but they're valuable all the same. They're more than a hundred years old. If you look at them carefully, you'll see Queen Victoria on there, wearing her hair in a bun. Goodnight now.'

She shut the door, and the two boys examined the coins under the nearest street lamp. They could just make out the shape of a young woman's head. They slipped the smooth coins into their pockets, and turned into the next drive.

'Colonel Savage lives here,' said Foxy. 'He's got a bulldog.'

'Oh, are you sure we want to call here then?' asked Imran. 'I don't fancy a savage bulldog.'

'No, Wellington's a soft old thing,' said Foxy. 'And he's daft as a brush.'

They walked up to the door and Foxy pulled the cord that hung down by the ship's bell – ding, ding, ding. A face peered out through the round window by the door, then the door opened and Colonel Savage stood there, his red face all smiles.

'I must say I like those masks,' he exclaimed,

before they could say anything. 'They remind me of some I saw in South America once. And now I suppose it's Trick or Treat time?'

The monsters nodded.

'Well, I was going to make treacle toffee – that seemed just the thing for Hallowe'en, but Wellington can't manage it without any teeth, you know, so I've made some mulled punch, piping hot, very cheering on a cold night – he likes a saucer of that – I'm quite partial to it myself, of course. Don't worry, there's no alcohol in it, I'm not allowed any – it's mostly fruit juice and cinnamon, but none the worse for that.'

He disappeared into the kitchen and the boys stared at Wellington's scowling face. Then Colonel Savage reappeared with two steaming mugs. The monsters pushed their masks up again and sipped the drink; it was hot and spicy.

'Mmm, delish,' said the Horrifibiter.

They finished their drinks, gave Wellington a nervous pat and said goodbye.

'I'm feeling quite full up,' said the Fierceychewemup.

'Let's do just one more,' said the Horrifibiter.

'Oh, all right – this is Mrs Reed's house,' said Foxy. 'She's really nice.'

They pulled their masks well down over their faces and rang the doorbell. Mrs Reed stood

there, wiping her hands on her apron. The light from the hall shone down on them.

'The sky is blue, the grass is green, have you got a penny for Hallowe'en?'

'Certainly not!' exclaimed Mrs Reed. 'I'm not having cheeky youngsters begging for money on my doorstep – be off with you.'

'Er . . . Trick or Treat then?' asked Imran, backing away.

'You'll get no treats from me, young man, coming here in nasty masks, frightening a poor old woman in the dark!'

The door slammed shut.

'I thought you said she was nice,' said Imran.

'She is usually,' said Foxy.

'I'm going to play a trick on her,' said Imran.

'Oh, no, Immy,' said Foxy. 'She *is* nice, honest, and she's a friend of ours.'

'Just a *little* trick,' insisted Imran.

He took a piece of chalk from his pocket and tiptoed to the wall near the front door. Along the bricks he scrawled:

'Mrs Reed is a real old meanie,
She wouldn't give a treat to a Halloweenie.'

'Hang on, Immy,' said Foxy. 'You can't leave that there.'

'Keep your hair on,' said Imran. 'The rain'll wash it off in no time. Now, shall we do some more houses?'

Foxy shook his head. He'd had enough for one night.

'See you Monday then,' called Imran, 'Bye,' and he ran off to his end of the street.

The following morning, just as Foxy was finishing his breakfast, there was a knock at the door. His mother went to answer it. He could hear the murmur of voices and his mother saying, 'Of course, of course.'

'That was Mrs Reed,' she said, coming back into the room.

Foxy swallowed his cereal the wrong way and choked. His mother thumped him on the back and went on:

'She says there's a little job she'd particularly like you to do for her, Foxy – so I said you'd pop round before doing my shopping, to see what she wants.'

Foxy forced himself to ring at Mrs Reed's front door. He kept his face turned away from the chalked scrawl on the bricks. He felt quite sick.

'Ah, Foxy,' smiled Mrs Reed. 'Just the sort of sensible lad I need. Do you see this?'

She waved her hand towards the chalked words.

'– A couple of young vandals visited me last night; they had masks on, so I couldn't see their faces, unfortunately. It was Mischief Night, you see, and when I refused to give them a treat, this is what they left me.'

Foxy scuffed the toe of his trainer on the step. Mrs Reed went on:

'Now you know I often get twinges of rheumatism, so I thought it would be easier for someone with young muscles to clean it off.

Here's a bucket of hot water, and here's some cleaning powder and a scrubbing brush – ring the bell when you've finished, and I'll come out and see what sort of a job you've made of it.'

Foxy was left with no choice in the matter. He scrubbed and scrubbed at the writing, poured scouring powder on to the brush and scrubbed away again until he was sweating all over with the effort. Eventually all the writing was rubbed off. Then he had to rinse the streaks of white powder off the bricks. His wet hands were red and sore in the biting wind. He rang Mrs Reed's doorbell and could hear her limping to open it.

'Ah, Foxy,' she said, looking at the wall, which was now dripping wet, but clean. 'You are a good boy; thank you very much. Now here's a bag of apples off my tree, I'm sure your family can make good use of them. Watch how you go now. Don't trip: your laces are undone.'

She smiled to herself as Foxy put down the bag of apples and bent to do up his laces.

'Do you know, Foxy,' she said, 'I'd recognize those red and black trainers anywhere.'

21

3

NOVEMBER

Remembrance

'Got any black shoe polish, Mum?' asked Foxy, opening and shutting cupboard doors in the kitchen.

'Under the sink with the brushes,' said his mother.

Foxy took the tin of polish and an old rag, and sat at the kitchen table.

'Is Mr Tucker having a shoe inspection or something?' asked his mother.

'No,' Foxy shook his head. 'It's for the parade on Sunday. They want the Cubs to be in it, too.'

'Oh, yes, of course,' she said. 'Then I'd better make sure your neckscarf is clean too.'

'I've never been on one of these parades before,' said Foxy. 'I don't know if I fancy all that marching about and standing in the cold.'

He put his hand inside a shoe and held it up to smooth polish into it. As he worked, he began to whistle tunelessly between his teeth.

There was a long ring at the doorbell. Foxy dropped everything and ran to see who it was. On the doorstep stood an elderly man in a tattered old jacket and muddy trousers tied round with string. Tufts of white hair stuck out from the sides of his grubby cap. He had a large box in his hands. Thomas stared at him.

''Lo, son,' he said. 'Your Gran in?'

'Oh, er, I'll get her,' said Foxy. 'Would you like . . . to come in?'

'No, son, I won't, thanks – my boots are covered in mud.'

Gran came downstairs smiling and took the box from the man.

'Thanks very much, Ratty,' she said. 'Is the tin in there as well?'

'Yes,' he nodded. 'And the list of streets – let me have it all back after the weekend.'

'Right,' she said. 'Good of you to bring it round, Ratty.'

Foxy watched the man walk to the front gate; he had a slight limp.

'How do you know that tramp, Gran?' he asked.

'He's not a tramp,' she laughed. 'That's just his working clothes – he works for the Council in Parks and Gardens. I've known Ratty since we were at school together. He's very well known round here – I'm surprised you've not seen me talking to him before.'

'Oh,' said Foxy. 'But why's he brought you a present then?'

'It's my tray of poppies,' said Gran. 'I'm going round selling them this evening. Want to come?'

They set out after tea. Foxy was holding the money tin with a slit in the top. Gran had the tray of poppies round her neck.

'You should take up ice-cream selling in the cinema, Mother,' said Mum.

Gran and Foxy took it in turns to knock on doors. As the door opened they followed the same routine.

'Hello,' said Gran. 'Would you like to buy a poppy?'

Then they would wait. Each house sent out a different mixture of smells and sounds. Each hallway gave them clues about the people who lived there: a jumble of prams and toys, an array of hanging plants, or a walking-stick and a dog's lead. Back came the customer – sometimes friendly, sometimes silent – and would push coins into Foxy's tin and take a poppy. Then on to the next house.

'What are the poppies for, anyway?' asked Foxy.

'Remembrance,' said Gran. 'In the First World

War there was a lot of fighting in France in fields of poppies, so now it's become a flower that reminds people of anyone who died in past wars.'

'What's the money for then?' asked Foxy, ringing the next doorbell.

'It goes to help old soldiers or their families,' said Gran. 'Ooer, I don't like the look of him.'

The muzzle of an Alsatian had suddenly appeared, pressed against the frosted glass of the door. Foxy jabbed the bell once more, then they scuttled out of the gate and shut it, watching to see what would happen. An elderly woman came round the side of the house, wiping her hands on her apron. She saw what they wanted and went back in to fetch her purse.

'I always give to this,' she said to Gran. 'I still reckon I'm lucky to be alive, you know. I lived near Dover all through the last war, and the bombing was something awful – anything they had left after bombing London, they'd get rid of on us as they went back across the Channel. The nights I've spent huddled under the stairs or in the shelter in the back garden! We never seemed to get a good night's sleep; you'd just get to bed, then the siren would go . . . you'd tumble downstairs, waiting for the planes to pass overhead, then another long wait . . . and at last they'd

come back. Then there'd be the sound of bombs a few miles away, or sometimes just a whistle, then a sort of thump . . . We'd be longing for the All Clear siren, then we'd stagger back to bed at dawn. Thank God that's all over.'

Gran was nodding sympathetically.

'I was in the Land Army myself,' she said. 'Out in the country. We were away from the Blitz, of course, but it wasn't an easy life, believe you me.'

'Oh, I know you girls worked hard,' said the woman.

'We did,' said Gran. 'It was no joke getting up at six on a winter's morning, trying to get turnips out of the ground that was white with frost – we had to chip them out like stones out of concrete ... And then get back to milk the cows before the farmer let us have breakfast!'

'Do you remember that awful dried egg?' said the woman; she was automatically pushing coin after coin into Foxy's tin as she talked.

'What about that whale-meat then?' said Gran. 'Dreadful old stuff, wasn't it? – like eating fish-flavoured leather.'

'And only one egg a week,' said the woman. 'That was all we were allowed, wasn't it? They'd never credit it now, would they?'

She and Gran went on like this for quite a while. Foxy watched the Alsatian trying to bite the frosted glass and getting annoyed because its nose was in the way.

'Well, we'd better be off,' said Gran at last, handing the woman a poppy. 'We've another few houses to do.'

'Nice meeting you,' said the woman. 'You must come round for a cup of tea and a chin-wag some time – I'll get my old ration books out and we'll have a laugh about old times.'

'Right,' said Gran. 'And I'll hunt out that snap of me driving a tractor.'

Foxy had had enough.

'This tin weighs a ton, Gran,' he said. 'Just feel.'

'Phew, yes,' said Gran. 'And there are only a few poppies left. Let's be getting back for a nice hot cup of tea.'

On Sunday morning Foxy was ready to set off for the parade. He looked very smart in his green Cub pullover. His neckscarf was straight for once – Mum had seen to that – and his black shoes were polished to a high gloss.

'Might see you at the War Memorial later,' said Gran as he left.

He went up the High Street and met Imran and the other Cubs there. They were soon joined by members of the Red Cross, Brownies, and other groups. A brass band began to play and the parade moved off. Behind the band marched rows of old soldiers; their backs were very straight as they swung along. The parade led round the square and down the High Street.

They halted opposite the church and stood in their groups round the War Memorial. This was a tall block of white stone with the names of hundreds of dead soldiers carved on it. Usually the road past the church was busy with traffic, but today it was unusually quiet. The band stopped playing. The church clock stood at eleven exactly. Suddenly everything fell silent. Everyone just stood.

One by one, several men and women stepped forward and laid wreaths of red poppies on the white steps of the War Memorial. Then there was another silence. A boy raised a bugle to his lips. The sound cut through the stillness. It was sad and beautiful at the same time. The notes died away . . .

Now the parade was over. Some people started to drift away; others stood about chatting quietly. Foxy suddenly spotted Gran walking up to the War Memorial. He went over to her.

'Hello, Gran,' he said. 'What've you come for?'

'I always come here on Remembrance Sunday,' she said. 'I like to remember my cousin, Tom. He was killed in the war . . . look –'

She ran her finger down the list of names.

'There he is: Thomas Soper. He was a lovely lad. He had thick ginger hair and freckles, just like yours – you remind me of him sometimes – like the way you whistle through your teeth when you're concentrating on something . . . He was a dreadful tease, was Tom . . . one Christmas party we had, I remember, he put a spoonful of jelly down my back . . . I wouldn't speak to him for weeks after that . . .'

She and Foxy walked slowly round the War Memorial, looking at the long lists of names on each side.

'Morning, Janey,' said a voice.

Foxy swung round. He'd never heard his Gran called that before. He stared at the elderly gentleman who'd spoken. His white hair was brushed smooth. He was wearing a smart navy suit with a white shirt and black tie. There was a poppy in his button-hole. Across one side of his jacket were rows of coloured ribbons, and beneath them hung several medals. Foxy's eyes widened as he recognized him.

'Why, good morning, Ratty,' said Gran.

'Good turn-out this morning,' he said.

'So there should be,' said Gran. ' "At the going down of the sun and in the morning we will remember them." '

Ratty sighed and nodded. He slanted his right hand to his head in a sort of salute.

'Bye for now,' he said, and limped off briskly up the High Street.

'Why do you call him Ratty, Gran?' asked Foxy.

'That's just his nickname,' said Gran. 'He was one of the Desert Rats – they were the troops in the Western Desert during the war. Our Tom was a Desert Rat too, in the same regiment as Ratty; they were good friends.'

She paused.

'What happened?' asked Foxy.

'Well,' said Gran, 'they were in the same tank one day. It went over a mine and was blown up. Tom was killed instantly, but Ratty was thrown clear, although he was badly wounded, of course.'

She sighed and stopped again. Foxy was trying to take it all in. He said:

'But why . . . why didn't you ever tell me about this before, Gran?'

His Gran looked at him and gave his shoulders a tight squeeze.

'Well,' she said, 'perhaps I didn't think you were old enough to understand.'

She ruffled his thick ginger hair.

'– But now I think you are,' she said.

4

DECEMBER

Panto

As soon as the Autumn half-term was over, everyone had begun looking forward to Christmas. Mr Tucker's class had even started discussing how to decorate their room.

'How about lots of snowballs, sir?' suggested Vic. 'We could hang them from the ceiling.'

'They'd melt,' complained Lucy. 'They'd drip on us, wouldn't they?'

'I meant made of cotton-wool, dum-dum,' said Vic.

'We could do it up like Santa's grotto,' said Imran.

'Yes, all sparkly, like, with a tree –'

'Yes, and you could dress up like Santa, sir, and dish out lots of presents –'

'Ho, hum,' said Mr Tucker, frowning. A picture flashed across his mind of the members of his class thudding on to his lap to whisper their Christmas wishes. 'No, not at all a good idea, I'm afraid – after all, you'd know I wasn't really Santa, wouldn't you? – and that would spoil the effect.'

'We could make it like a panto – you know, sir, like in that story, the Sleeping Beauty. This classroom could be the castle –'

'Yes, and we could all be asleep –'

'Like in maths lessons –'

'Yeah, they last a hundred years sometimes –'

'Enough!' barked Mr Tucker. 'Let's keep our minds on our Christmas plans, shall we?'

Eventually it was settled that the room should be decorated in the traditional way: a large Nativity scene along one wall, then a Christmas tree, paperchains, coloured lanterns, lots of artificial snow, sparkle and glitter. But their Big Effort was to be put into the production of a pantomime: they decided on Cinderella.

The whole class helped with the writing; each scene was written by a different group.

'What rhymes with "slipper"?' puzzled Foxy.

' "Kipper," ' said Imran.

'Hmm,' frowned Foxy, chewing his pencil. 'We'd better think of another way of putting it – how about this for the Prince to say:

'Sit here, my dear, in dainty pose,
Let's try this slipper on your –'

'Nose,' said Imran.

Foxy glared at him and they both collapsed in guffaws. Mr Tucker's voice was heard above the hubbub of playwriting.

'We'll settle the final version on Friday, then decide on who's to play the parts – and we'll start rehearsing in earnest on Monday.'

Helen Bunting with the drip-dry hair seemed the obvious choice for Cinderella. Toothy Beddoes claimed the part of Prince Charming, because he had a satin suit he'd worn as a pageboy at his sister's wedding. Shamila Singh was to be the Fairy Godmother because it was quite a long part and she had a good memory for poetry.

('This is poetry?' said Mr Tucker.)

None of the girls fancied being labelled as an Ugly Sister, so Foxy and Imran found themselves chosen by their classmates.

'But why us?' protested Foxy.

'You must have the looks for it,' said Kevin Wilson.

Foxy leant over and punched him – but he wasn't really displeased. He rather fancied being in a panto. His mother was enthusiastic.

'We'll make your costume,' she said. 'Won't we, Gran?'

'I've got a really horrible old black wig you can have,' said Gran. 'Don't know why I ever bought it – it looks like a dead cat draped over my head.'

'Oh – thanks, Gran,' said Foxy.

Rehearsals were held regularly. Everyone in the class was involved, either on stage or behind the scenes. As the end of term drew near, the day of the Grand Panto was fixed. They were to perform it on stage in the School Hall. Meanwhile, they were busy designing and printing programmes, selling tickets and painting scenery. The cast knew their lines – just about – and costumes were ready.

'Now are you sure you've got all the props on that list?' Mr Tucker asked Tommy Pugh, the properties manager.

'Yes, sir, except for the white mice – Toby's bringing his two in tomorrow.'

'Mmm,' said Mr Tucker. 'Well, I can't really believe everything is going according to plan . . . though at the moment it seems like it.'

The Big Day arrived. The audience came in chattering excitedly. Behind the stage curtains, Mr Tucker's class were beginning to feel nervous.

'Think I can feel a nose-bleed coming on, sir,' reported Benjy, who was in charge of the lighting.

'Rubbish,' insisted Mr Tucker. 'Use your will-power: tell it to stop. But just make sure you have a big hanky with you.'

'The hall's full,' hissed Marlene, who had been standing with her eyes to a slit between the curtains.

'Right,' said Mr Tucker. 'Ready, everyone? Cinderella, get into position.'

Helen went and stood by the fireplace and put on her forlorn expression. The curtains opened; the audience fell silent. Helen began in a clear voice.

'I'm all alone with work to do –
Polish, dust and hoover through,
Do the washing, iron it, too,
Change the beds and clean the loo –
It's all too much for me to do . . .'

Then she began to weep. Foxy could see Betsy sitting wide-eyed in the audience; the story was easy enough for her to follow. Then the Ugly Sisters flounced on. It had taken nearly an hour to get their make-up gruesome enough; Foxy hoped his false nose wouldn't come unstuck. He glared at Cinderella and rapped out:

'Come on, Cinders, clear this mess!'
'Cinders, come and help me dress,' ordered the other Ugly Sister.
'Look at the state you've left this floor.'

'The coal's all gone – just fetch some more.'
'Unblock this drain, there's such a stench –
You really are a useless wench.'
'Get cracking, girl, your work's not done –
We're off to the Ball to have some fun!'

At last they paraded out, to loud applause,
leaving poor Cinderella alone again and even
more forlorn. In swept Shamila dressed in silver
foil and sparkly tinsel.

'Ooh,' gasped the little ones.

'Why, Cinders, what's the matter, dear? –
Your Fairy Godmother is here.'

Cinderella sobbed out her story. Her Fairy
Godmother was kindness itself:

'Bring me a pumpkin, bring me mice –
We'll get you transport in half a trice.'

Tommy Pugh had searched in every local
greengrocer's for pumpkins, but without success, so Cinderella fetched the swede turnip he
had ready for her. Then she fetched the cage of
mice Toby had brought. Helen wasn't too keen
on mice, and she plonked the cage down at Fairy
Godmother's feet with rather a bump. Fairy
Godmother began:

'I'll wave my wand just once, and then
The magic starts . . . please count to ten!'

The audience obediently began to count:
'One – two –'
The cage door swung open. Cinderella gave a
piercing shriek as one mouse streaked off. The
other hesitated, getting its bearings. Fairy Godmother was quick-thinking enough to whip off
her pointed hat and slam it down over the hesitant mouse. She grabbed the poor creature and
shoved it back in the cage. There was no sign of
the other one. She glared at Cinderella, who was
standing on tiptoe, looking petrified.
'– Six – seven –' chanted the audience.
Cinderella had picked up the turnip and the
cage and dashed off stage with them.

'– Nine – TEN!' yelled the audience.

Fairy Godmother looked towards the side of the stage. There wasn't a sign of movement. Had they all gone home? She kept her cool and turned to the audience.

'I'll ... er ... wave my wand once more, and then, I'll get you all to count to ten ... again,'

she said brightly.

'One – two –'

Fairy Godmother looked desperately towards the wings.

'Three – four –'

'Come on, come on,' she hissed out of the corner of her mouth. '*Do* something in there ...'

'Nine – TEN!'

In rolled Cinderella dressed in a shimmering gown, sitting upright in an old pram hidden by gold draperies. The audience cheered. Fairy Godmother beamed a smile of relief. The curtains closed for the interval. The audience applauded wildly. Backstage there was busy confusion.

'Phew,' said Mr Tucker, wiping his brow. 'Not bad, not bad at all – Well done, Fairy Godmother, I was proud of you. Now where did that second mouse get to?'

'I keep calling it, sir,' said Toby, crawling

across the stage, 'but it's not very well trained yet.'

Mr Tucker looked at him sourly.

'Well, just keep looking,' he said.

Dancers were positioning themselves ready for the Ball. Scene-shifters grunted as they hauled a grandfather clock to the back of the ballroom. Toothy Beddoes was having trouble with his satin suit; it was definitely too small for him.

'You didn't say you were a page-boy *three years ago*,' protested Sylvia, trying to pin it together across his chest. 'Oh, spit! – there goes another button – look, you'll have to wear this tinsel draped across like a scarf to hide the joins.'

'Ready?' hissed Mr Tucker. 'Cinderella? Prince Charming? – oh, my gosh, what a sight – never mind, yes, just don't breathe . . .'

The curtains opened to waltz music. Everyone was dancing and supposed to be having a wonderful time. Prince Charming was stiff at dancing at the best of times; now it seemed that he had four left feet and was doing a robot impression. Cinderella managed to haul him round the stage.

'Eeeeeeeaah!' Cinderella gave a high-pitched scream and leapt at Prince Charming, clinging round his neck with her feet off the floor. The prince staggered.

'Gerroff, gerroff!' he yelled. 'Sir, gederoff!'

'Mouse!' she screamed.

'Eeek! . . . Where? . . . Help!'

Her panic was infectious, and the stately dance broke up in confusion as everyone scattered and peered at the stage. Among their legs, Toby could be seen on hands and knees, like a hound on the scent.

'Got him!' he cried, holding the struggling mouse above his head like a well-held catch. He disappeared off stage with it. The music continued. Cinderella let go of Prince Charming, whose suit had fallen completely apart and was hanging off his shoulders. He glared furiously at

Cinderella. Jason came on with a gong. He stood in front of the clock and pushed its hands to twelve. Doinng! Doinng! . . . Cinderella pulled away from the Prince and managed to remember her next lines:

'The clock is striking, midnight's near,
My night out's over now, I fear.'

She staggered towards the steps, pulling off one of her tinselly gym shoes as she went. Prince Charming clutched the remains of his jacket in one hand and pointed stiffly at the steps.

'What's this I spy? – A slipper fine? –
The girl who dropped it shall be mine;
It sparkles with a brilliant glitter,
If I can find her, it will fit her . . .'

Off he went, followed by the dancers, to a great round of applause. The next scene was back in Cinderella's house. The Ugly Sisters were screeching at one another:

'This dainty slipper fits my foot –
I tell you that it's mine, you brute!'
'You lying toad, you must be blind –
My foot's the one they want to find.'

At last Cinderella was brought in. Prince Charming went stiffly down on one knee. There was a loud ripping sound as his trouser seams split. Cinderella sniggered.

'Shurrup, you,' growled the Prince.

His courtiers stood with their shoulders shaking. Suddenly the stage lights went blue; everyone looked ghastly and ghostly. Mr Tucker's voice could be heard behind the scenes.

'What's the matter back there?'

A voice came from the lighting corner:

'Benjy hit the wrong switch, sir – he's having a nose-bleed.'

There was a brief pause, then normal lighting returned. Action began again. Prince Charming managed to wedge the gym shoe on to Cinderella's foot.

'Ouch,' she said. 'Watch it.'

He glared at her, saying:

'I've thought of nothing but your beauty,
Will you be mine, you little cutey?'

Rubbing her toes, Cinderella replied in a sulky tone:

'At last my fondest dream's come true:
I want to spend my life with you . . .'

The curtains jerked shut again.

'You clumsy lummock,' snapped Cinderella to the Prince. 'You nearly had my little toe off.'

'You shouldn't have such big feet then, should you?' he snapped back.

'Never mind that now, you love-birds,' said Mr Tucker. 'Get ready for the wedding.'

Someone found a cloak to drape round Prince Charming and cover his state of undress. Cinderella put on a veil and tiara. Fairy Godmother tried to pull her hat back to a point – it was looking very scrumpled after being used as a mousetrap. At last the courtiers, Ugly Sisters and the rest were ready. The curtains opened. The stage was brilliantly lit with strings of twinkling fairy lights.

'Aaaahh,' said the audience, clapping.

The wedding took place and Prince Charming led his bride, limping slightly, to the front for applause. Courtiers strewed them with confetti. Suddenly all the lights went off, flickered on again, went off, then came on again. The audience thought it was all part of the effects and cheered even more.

The cast curtseyed and bowed. Foxy's dead-cat wig fell off at his feet – more cheers. Toby came on and held the mouse's cage up like a lantern – loud applause for the mice. Mr Tucker squeezed in at the back. He pulled on Benjy, whose face was completely hidden by the red-streaked hanky clamped over his nose – more cheers for

Benjy's nose. The cast curtseyed and bowed yet again. The audience cheered and whistled. The curtains jerked shut. The audience was still clapping.

'Encore – more, more!' they were calling.

'They must be mad,' said Mr Tucker.

'Oh, sir, why not more?' begged the cast, flushed with success. 'Why not next year, sir – one of those mega-productions – you know, sir – with a cast of thousands . . .?'

'Over my dead body,' said Mr Tucker.

5

JANUARY

Snow

Foxy stood with the saw in his hand and watched snowflakes settling on the playground outside. If it kept on at this rate, there'd be quite a thick layer by home-time.

'Come on, Foxy,' urged Mr Tucker. 'I thought that coffee table was a Christmas present for your Gran – it's the second week of January already.'

'It's the legs,' frowned Foxy, turning back to the workbench. 'It's taking me ages to get them exactly the same length.'

Mr Tucker picked up the little table and examined it.

'Well, you will keep sawing bits off . . . those legs are certainly shorter than when you started this, back in November,' he said. 'But you've given it a very nice smooth finish, and I like the pattern of roses you've painted on it. Perhaps it's time you took it home anyway, then you can start something new.'

'Oh, great,' said Foxy, in a relieved voice. 'Gran's still waiting for her mystery Christmas present.'

At home-time Foxy held the finished coffee table sideways under his arm. Imran joined him and they crunched across the snowy playground.

'What've you got there?' asked Imran.

'It's that coffee table I've been making for Gran,' said Foxy.

'The legs are a bit short, aren't they?' asked Imran. He put his head on one side and thought about the table.

'I suppose your Gran could turn it into a skateboard,' he said.

Splat!

A snowball thudded into Imran's back. He whirled round, lost his balance and grabbed at Foxy's arm. Foxy's feet shot from under him and they both landed on the ground. The table skidded away. The boys struggled to their feet, looking round angrily.

Splat!

A second snowball hit Foxy on the side of his head, knocking off his woolly hat. Snow fell icily inside his collar.

'Eugh,' he exclaimed furiously, clawing at the

wet snow to get rid of it. 'Who did that?'

'They're behind the wall,' said Imran, brushing the snow out of his black hair so that it stood up in spikes. 'It could be that lot in Class 3.'

He picked up a handful of snow and threw it at the spot where the snowballs had come from, but it fell harmlessly against the wall.

'Come on,' said Foxy, 'I don't want to fight now, I want to get this table home in one piece.'

They made their way down the road as fast as they could on the slippery pavement. Half a dozen snowballs thudded into their backs as they slithered away.

'Just wait until tomorrow,' said Foxy. 'Then we'll be ready for them.' He said goodbye to Imran and went into the house. As he stamped the snow off his shoes, Betsy came running out to him. She flung her arms round his legs.

'What's that?' she asked, pointing at the table.

'It's Gran's Christmas present,' said Foxy. 'It's a table.'

Betsy took one look at the table and ran in to Gran.

'Foxy's got a boat for you,' she shouted. 'It's a boat.'

'Happy late Christmas, Gran,' said Foxy, setting the little table down beside her.

'Oh, Foxy, that's beautiful,' said Gran. 'And

the top all painted with roses – you *are* a clever boy.'

'I know it's a little bit low down,' said Foxy, 'but I kept sawing the legs shorter to try to even them up.'

Gran put her hand on it and it wobbled a little.

'Doesn't matter a bit if it's not quite straight,' she said. 'Think of the leaning tower of Pisa – people come from all over the world to look at that.'

'It's not a table, it's a boat,' said Betsy firmly.

She got hold of the little table and pulled it over on to its side, then completely upside down, so that its stumpy legs stuck up in the air. She stepped inside and stamped her feet with glee, holding two of the legs to steer with.

'Brrmm-brrmm,' she said delightedly. 'It's my boat.'

That night everything froze. When Foxy walked to school the next morning, the snow was crunchy and slippery under his feet, and he stamped on all the ice-covered puddles to hear the cracks and squeaks.

At play-time he and Imran and some of the others made a good long slide which stretched half-way across the playground. By home-time it was bitterly cold again; the sun was a glowing red ball in a grey sky. They all wanted to get home as fast as they could. Foxy pulled his woolly hat down over his ears. He and Imran hurried along as fast as they could, slipping and sliding by the hedge.

Then, just as they walked underneath some overhanging branches, splat! – a well-aimed snowball thudded into the middle of the bushes and shook down a shower of snow right on to the boys' heads. They were bewildered for a moment or two, and then more snowballs came flying at them from behind the opposite hedge, hitting them on the arms and chest. The last one sent Foxy's woolly hat spinning into the bushes.

'Right, that's it!' shouted Foxy. 'Get the ammo, Immy!'

With lightning speed they made half a dozen snowballs and lobbed them over the road to land behind the hedge. They were satisfied when they heard cries of 'Yeugh' and 'Eeogh,' and knew they'd found their targets. They followed up the first attack by sending another half dozen sailing over the hedge. The few which came back their way just landed harmlessly in the middle of the road. A few moments later they heard the slithering sound of footsteps growing fainter in the distance.

'Cowards,' said Imran. 'They wouldn't even come out into the open.'

Foxy didn't answer; he was searching under the bushes for his woolly hat. Suddenly he stopped.

'What's the matter?' asked Imran.

Foxy stood up slowly. Cupped in his hands was a little bird. It was lying motionless, its eyes shut. They looked at it for a moment or two, watching for signs of life.

'It must have died of cold,' said Imran eventually.

'Poor little thing,' whispered Foxy.

Perhaps it was the sound of their voices, but the little bird's eyelids fluttered . . . then shut again.

'It's still alive,' said Foxy.

He picked up his knitted hat and gently lowered the soft little body into it. The boys set off for home.

'Seeya,' called Imran, turning into the entrance of his house. Foxy walked the rest of the way with one hand holding the top of the hat and the other hand supporting it underneath. He thought the warmth from his hand might be unthawing the tiny body inside.

'That you, Foxy?' called his mother.

'Ssshhh,' said Foxy. 'Look what I've got.'

She peered inside the hat, then Gran and Betsy came and looked.

'Aaahh,' they all said. 'Poor little thing.'

'Where can we put it to keep it warm?' asked Foxy.

'In the boat,' said Betsy, her eyes shining. 'In the boat.'

She pulled Foxy towards the corner near the fire, where Gran's new table was standing upside down, lined with a piece of blanket. Five dolls were propped up inside. Betsy yanked the dolls up by the legs and threw them over her shoulder. Then she crouched down, waiting for

Foxy. Why not? he thought. He gently scooped up the bird and laid it in the blankets. Its eyelids fluttered again, and its beak opened and shut. Foxy had never seen a bird from so close before. The top of its head was blue, like its beak and tail; its chest was a soft yellow. The feathers on its face were white, with a black line from the top of its beak to the side of its head.

'It's a blue-tit,' said Foxy's Mum. 'Aren't its colours beautiful?'

All through that evening, they watched the blue-tit. It gradually seemed to come to life, opening and shutting its beak more frequently and blinking its beady eyes. Foxy's mother brought in the tops of two jam jars.

'This one's got warm sugary water in,' she said. 'He might like to sip it when he's more lively. This one's got some crumbs and bits of nuts I've chopped up very small.'

Foxy gently held the blue-tit so that its beak could touch the water. It moved its beak once or twice, but they couldn't tell if it drank any.

By the time Foxy went to bed, the blue-tit was no longer lying helpless on its side, but was standing a little unsteadily on its own feet. When he crept downstairs early the next morning and switched on the light, the bird gave a soft twitter as though to greet him. Foxy noticed that some of the nut and crumb mixture had gone – the little bird seemed to be recovering fast.

'I think you'd better let it go today,' said Mum. She saw the disappointed looks on the children's faces. 'Otherwise it may start to fly round inside and bump into the windows in panic and perhaps hurt its wings – it's a little wild bird, don't forget: it needs to be free to fly where it wants to.'

'But it might freeze again,' said Foxy.

'I think it was hungry as well as cold,' said Mum. 'If birds can eat well, that helps to keep them strong, then they don't feel the cold so badly.'

Foxy looked out at the garden, which was still hidden under deep snow. He imagined his little blue-tit trying to find food in that cold white wilderness.

'We ought to clear a special space to put food out for it, so it knows where to come,' he said.

'Yes,' said Mum. 'We ought to have a bird-table.'

'Gran's got a table,' said Betsy through a mouthful of toast.

'You can borrow it if you like,' said Gran.

As it was Saturday and Foxy didn't have to go to school, he disappeared into the shed with Gran's coffee table. Later that morning the sound

of banging echoed round the garden. Betsy raced to the window.

'Ooh, look,' she said. 'A table for the birds.'

Foxy had glued the little table to the flat top of an old fence post. Now he was banging the whole thing down into a hole he had managed to dig out of the frozen ground. It took quite a time, but eventually it stood upright and steady. His mother took him out some more of the crumb and nut mixture, as well as some chopped-up

56

cheese-rind and apple. He sprinkled it on top of the new bird-table. Then he went indoors and fetched the blue-tit.

Everyone watched as Foxy placed it on top of the table. It pecked once or twice at the food. Then it seemed to gather all its strength together and flew off into the nearest bushes.

'Bye, bye, Bluey,' called Betsy, waving.

'He'll be back,' said Mum. 'As soon as he feels hungry again he'll find his way back to our bird-table.'

'Yes, course he will,' said Gran.

'And it'll be easy for him to find,' said Foxy, 'because I bet it's the only bird-table in the world with roses painted on the top.'

6

FEBRUARY

Shrove Tuesday

'Ouch – look out!'

'Ooh, sorry,' exclaimed Foxy, staggering back. He had turned the corner of the street and run straight into a jogger in a green and white track suit. She scowled at him, breathing heavily, then got back into her jogging rhythm and padded off again. Foxy ran up the path and into the kitchen.

'Hi, Mum, wassfotea?' he asked all in one breath.

'Hello, love, beefburger and beans,' she said. 'But you can get yourself a glass of milk just for now – I'll be organized in a few minutes.'

She was standing in the middle of the kitchen, looking at the heaps of dirty washing all round her on the floor.

'The man came to mend the washing machine and he's only just left, so I'll try and get this load going before I make the tea.'

Foxy poured himself a glass of milk and sat

down to drink it. He watched his mother loading the washing machine with clothes: Gran's, Dad's, her own, lots of Betsy's vests and T-shirts, his own underwear and shirts –

'Where are your football shorts, Foxy?' asked his Mum. 'They might as well go in too – they're supposed to be white, after all.'

'They're still in my bag,' he said; he was too tired to move. 'Here, Betsy – take my bag to Mum.'

Betsy came over to him, beaming, and hugged his school bag to her chest. She staggered across to Mum and dropped it at her feet. Mum unzipped it and felt around inside for the football shorts.

'Eugh – what on earth have you got in here, Foxy?' she asked. 'Bits of stones –'

'No, they're fossils,' he protested.

'And bits of old bone –'

'No, Mum, that's a mouse's skull.'

'And a handful of grass –'

'No, no, there's a four-leaved clover in that, Mum – a four-leaved clover is lucky. I found it on the school field today when we were snail-hunting. It's for you; it'll bring you good luck tomorrow.'

'Well, thank you, dear – but why should I need good luck specially for tomorrow?'

'In the race, Mum, in the parents' Pancake Race . . .'

There was a long silence.

'Foxy,' said Mum, too quietly, 'you've done it again, haven't you? – forgotten to give me a letter from school.'

She scrabbled about among the brown apple cores and other rubbish in the bottom of his school bag, and found a tattered piece of paper. She unfolded it and read the letter. There was to be a Parents' Pancake Race on the school field at eleven o'clock on Pancake Tuesday –

'Tomorrow!' cried Mum. 'And this is the first I've heard about it. Oh, Foxy, you should have told me – I can't go in for it, I've got too much to do, and besides – I haven't run for years.'

'But you used to be a good runner, Mum, we've got photos of you in shorts.'

'Yes, but –'

'And anyway, Mr Tucker wanted the names in today, so I've put you down already.'

'Foxy!' she shrieked. Then she shrugged, 'Ah, well – what the heck . . .'

She started the washer, then reached for the tin opener and frying pan. 'Beefburger and beans, is it then?' she asked.

She started the cooking, then went to see what Gran wanted in the next room.

'Can you just check these stitches for me, dear?' asked Gran, glancing up from her knitting. 'I can't seem to get it right – I've counted seventy-nine stitches three times and there should be eighty.'

'Well – all right – quickly, then – I'm just getting Foxy's tea . . .'

But by the time Mum returned to the smoky kitchen, treading through the washing powder Betsy had poured on to the floor, the beefburgers looked like shrivelled black biscuits – and the state of the frying pan was indescribable.

'Oh, what the heck,' said Mum again. 'You don't mind beans on their own, do you, Foxy?'

At ten to eleven the next morning, all the children were out on the school field. They stood on either side of the grass track where the parents were going to run. The starting line was behind the kitchens, and the finishing line was just past the big oak tree in the middle of the field. The competitors began to line up. One enormous man in a blue string vest had tattoos all the way up his arms.

'That's my Dad, he's dead strong, he's bound to win,' said Kevin.

'Why should he, just 'cause he's strong?' demanded Shamila. 'Not all strong people are good runners.'

'My Mum's going to wear a four-leaved clover for luck,' said Foxy.

'*My* Mum's been jogging for weeks to get in trim,' said Kath. 'Look, there she is – in the green and white track suit – doesn't she look confident?'

Foxy recognized the jogger, who did indeed look very confident. She was doing warming-up exercises: swinging down to touch her left foot with her right hand and her right foot with her left hand, then swinging upright and trotting on the spot. Imran's Dad was talking to Foxy's Mum, who had dressed up as a waitress in a black dress and a white apron. She hadn't been able to clean the frying-pan properly – not even by chipping off the burnt bits – so it matched the colour of her dress. The pancake she had prepared was rather grey, speckled with bits of black – but, as she had said to Foxy beforehand, no one judged runners by the colour of their pancakes, and he'd had to agree. She saw Foxy and gave him a secret wave. Gran was on the side-line, holding Betsy up to watch. Foxy went over to say Hello to them. Gran nodded across at the competitors.

'I see they "stand like greyhounds in the slips, straining upon the start",' she said, in what Foxy knew was her poetry voice.

Mr Tucker was standing ready with the starting pistol.

'Ladies and gentlemen,' he announced, 'you must run with your frying pan from here to the finishing line. As you run, you must toss your pancake at least three times and catch it in the pan. If you drop it, you must go back and start the race again. Will you line up, please?'

The twenty or so Mums and Dads got ready on the starting line.

'Ready, steady –'

Bang! went the starting pistol. The competitors set off at a great rate. The children began to cheer their parents on. Kath's mother sprang forward with long strides. Imran's Dad sprinted off looking athletic. Kevin's Dad thundered along; the frying pan looked just like a spoon in his great fist. Foxy's Mum darted forward nimbly, tossing the pancake as she went. She had soon tossed it three times and then put on a spurt to overtake most of the others, who had dropped theirs or were laughing so much they couldn't go on.

Kevin's Dad tossed his pancake for the second time and it landed on the grass; he muttered 'Shucks,' and pounded back to the start with it. Lucy's dog, Andrex, appeared from nowhere, lolloped on to the field and jumped up at Imran's

Dad, who fell over backwards with Andrex, the frying pan and the pancake on top of him.

'Oh, no!' groaned Imran.

Now Foxy's Mum and the Jogger were ahead of all the rest. The Jogger still had her last toss to make. As they raced towards the oak tree, she tossed it for the third time. It sailed up in the air – but didn't come down again.

'It's stuck in the tree,' wailed Kath.

Foxy's Mum shot past the Jogger and reached the finishing line first.

'My Mum's won!' shouted Foxy, leaping about and waving his arms in the air. 'Good old Mum – that's the four-leaved clover, it brought her luck.'

'But I gave my Dad one as well,' complained Imran, 'and he hasn't won.'

'Oh,' said Foxy. 'Well, maybe mine was fresher than yours. Look, she's going to get a prize.'

The children and the rest of the competitors cheered as Foxy's Mum was presented with her prize. Foxy cheered and laughed – the prize was a non-stick frying pan. Mum saw Foxy and waved both her frying pans at him in triumph.

'Un-burnt beefburger and beans for tea?' she asked.

'No – pancakes, please,' said Foxy.

7

MARCH

Mother's Day

It was Friday afternoon. Mr Tucker was giving his class what he called 'a briefing' about what they would be doing the following week. Foxy was hardly listening; he was watching the wind pick up the leaves and crisp-papers and swirl them round the corners of the playground.

'So bring in a twenty-pence piece each for the ingredients,' said Mr Tucker. 'And you can each make a box of peppermint creams.'

'Peppermint creams?'

Foxy wondered whether he had heard right – what did peppermint creams have to do with school?

'What do we want to make them for?' he whispered to Imran.

'Mother's Day,' Imran whispered back. 'It's a week on Sunday.'

'Don't forget to bring some sort of box to pack them in,' Mr Tucker reminded them. 'A tea-bag box, perhaps, or a cake box, then you can cover it with decorated paper.'

Foxy didn't really want to make peppermint creams; he wasn't very good at making things, and anyway, he wanted to give his mother something better than that – something really big and super . . . a home computer with a set of games, or a BMX perhaps, or an Action Man – the possibilities were endless. He would have to start saving money.

During the next few days, Foxy knocked on all the doors in the street, offering to do odd jobs. The first was cleaning Mr Porrett's car. It was a cold day, but Foxy worked away, sponging and soaping and rinsing off. When Betsy looked out of the window and saw what he was doing, she screamed angrily because Mum wouldn't allow her to help him: wearing wellies and throwing water all over everything looked fun. Foxy polished the headlights, rearlights and bumpers, and Mr Porritt was so pleased he gave him fifty pence.

Then Mrs Mundy across the road saw what a good job he'd made and asked him to wash her Mini; she gave him fifty pence, too. He came home pleased with himself, and very wet and grimy.

'It's a good thing all your clothes are old

clothes,' said his Mum. At bed-time she took his
shirt, trousers and socks, and threw them
straight in the washing machine.

The next day Foxy took Colonel Savage's dog
for a run and weeded Mrs Mundy's garden bor-
der. Now he had two twenty-pence pieces. The
knees of his trousers were green from kneeling
on the grass, but when he undressed for bed, his
Mum just threw his dirty clothes in the washing
machine. Next day old Mrs Bell, who was a little
hard of hearing, asked him to polish several old
brass jugs. That took ages, but they gleamed like
gold when he had finished rubbing away at
them.

'It's a pity I'm not Aladdin,' he joked to her.

'But you *are* allowed in – any time you like,
dear,' she said.

She gave him a pound coin. On the next few evenings, he did more jobs after school: polished six pairs of shoes for Colonel Savage, cleaned all the downstairs windows for Mrs Reed, fetched shopping for Mrs Mundy, and helped Mr Johnson clean out his greenhouse and wash all the plant-pots. Every night, his mother just threw his grimy clothes into the washing machine; she was glad he was keeping so busy.

On Thursday, after he had helped Mrs Bell sort out her shed, his Gran called him into her room.

'Hey, you look a bit grubby,' she exclaimed, eyeing his cobwebby hair and dusty clothes. 'Now, how's the cash situation, Foxy?'

He fetched the margarine tub he kept his savings in and counted it out in front of her . . . four pounds, eighty pence.

'Well, I'll give you another twenty pence to make it five pounds,' she said. 'Then, if you give me all that change, I'll give you a five-pound note for it – there you are.'

They exchanged the money, and Foxy found himself holding a crisp five-pound note. It was the first he had ever owned. He examined it carefully: a picture of the Queen on one side and Wellington on the other (how was it he had the same name as Colonel Savage's dog?). Foxy folded it and pushed it down into the pocket of his dusty green shirt.

'I suppose all this odd-jobbing is to earn money for Mother's Day?' asked Gran.

'How did you guess, Gran?' he asked.

A knowing look crossed her face and she tapped the side of her nose with her finger.

'I'm a Mum too, you know,' she said. 'I remember your Dad getting up to just the same sort of things when he was your age. But of course in those days, flowers were only about a shilling a bunch; that's five pence in today's money.'

'Oh, do you think flowers would be best? They don't seem very interesting.'

'All mothers love flowers,' Gran assured him firmly.

Foxy supposed he'd better take her advice; he would buy them on Saturday, the day before Mother's Day. Gran said she would hide them for him in her wardrobe until the Sunday morning.

'So now that's all settled hunkydory – will you scratch my back for me, dear?' she asked. 'I've got the most dreadful itch, and I can't reach it . . . that's right, up a bit . . . yes, now down to the left, rub hard, *hard*, yes, that's lovely . . . now a bit more to the right, a good hard scratch – I want my twenty pence worth!'

When Foxy went out of Gran's room, his Mum spotted him and insisted on his having a bath immediately and washing his hair to get the cobwebs out. Meanwhile, she threw all his dusty clothes into the washing machine.

The next day was Friday. In the afternoon Mr Tucker helped his class make the peppermint creams.

'It's dead easy this, isn't it?' said Imran, as they rolled small balls of the mixture, then flattened them with a piece of cardboard. They put each sweet into a sweet-paper and placed them in a box.

'Have you tasted this?' whispered Foxy. 'It's scrummy.'

They each put a fingerful of the mixture into their mouths, where it melted deliciously. But Mr Tucker missed nothing, and the two boys finished up making the rest of their sweets with him standing over them, watching every movement like a hawk.

When Foxy got home, his mother was in the kitchen ironing. Keeping the box of sweets behind his back, he sidled past her, rushed to his bedroom and shut the door. He hid the box under his pillow and looked for the margarine tub to check his flower-money again. But the tub was empty! His heart thumped with panic – until he remembered that he'd given Gran the change, and she had given him a five-pound note – and he'd put it somewhere safe . . .

But where? Where had he put it? He tried to remember . . . Ah! Into his pocket, his shirt pocket, his *shirt pocket*! – And his mother had thrown all his dirty clothes into the washer! He thundered downstairs to the kitchen.

'Mum, Mum, where's my green sh-shirt?' he stammered out.

'What's the panic?' she asked. 'It's here in the pile; I'm just going to iron it.'

'But what about my money?'

'What money?'

'My savings – my five pounds – it was in the pocket.'

Horrified, Foxy's mother tweaked the green shirt from the washing basket and held it out to him. He thrust his hand down inside the pocket – and pulled out a carefully folded, soggy five-pound note. He couldn't say a word, he was so relieved. He just held it out to his mother. She took the crumpled note from him and placed it carefully on the ironing board and flattened it out. Then she pulled a hanky from the washing and spread it over the note. She pressed the iron down. There was a hiss and a cloud of steam.

Foxy's stomach turned over – suppose the note fell into little scraps of wet paper . . . all his savings . . . all that hard work . . . all the money he needed for his Mum's present . . .

'There you are,' she said. 'That still looks like a fiver to me. Keep it flat and put it somewhere warm to dry.'

Hardly believing his good luck, Foxy tip-toed along to his bedroom with the five-pound note lying on the palm of his hand. He laid it flat on the window-sill and waited for it to dry.

While he sat there on his bed, he took the box of peppermint creams from under his pillow. He opened it and looked at them. He counted them . . . nineteen . . . twenty. A delicious fragrance of peppermint reached his nostrils. He picked up one of the sweets, to see if it was perfectly round. One side of it was a little flattened, so he nibbled it to even it up again. Then he nibbled it a little more to make sure it was as pepperminty as the bit he had tasted in class. It looked rather small by then, so he finished it and rearranged the others in the box, so that they still filled it . . .

Half an hour later he looked up to see that his five-pound note was completely dry. The next day he bought a beautiful bunch of irises and daffodils. The florist put them inside a transparent bag and tied them with a blue bow. Foxy

took them home and smuggled them into Gran's room, where she hid them in the wardrobe.

On the morning of Mother's Day, Foxy's Dad took Gran, and then Mum, a cup of tea in bed. Betsy stood excitedly at the side of the bed, pushing Mum's eyelids open with her fingers. Mum struggled to sit up in bed. Then Foxy marched in with both hands behind his back.

'Happy Mother's Day,' he said and presented her with the flowers. She was really pleased, he could see that. Then he handed her the box of sweets.

'Mmm – what a pretty box, Foxy,' she said,

'and – oh, peppermint creams inside – lovely: eight yummy peppermint creams.'

'Oh, er . . . yes, there were one or two more,' said Foxy. 'But they looked a bit squashed, so I . . . um . . . took them out.'

'Very thoughtful, too,' said Mum.

She gave Betsy and Dad and Gran a peppermint, and took one for herself. She offered the box to Foxy. He shook his head.

'No, thanks, Mum – I've sort of gone off them.'

His Mum took the paper off the flowers to look at them properly.

'Are you sure you wouldn't rather have had an Action Man or one of those radio-controlled tanks or something?' asked Foxy anxiously.

'Oh, no,' said Mum. 'Spring flowers and sweets – what more could I want?'

8

APRIL

Easter

It was the last day of the Easter term – and it was one of those mornings when everything goes wrong. Betsy had been playing with the alarm clock the day before and had switched off the alarm, so Mum woke up later than usual. She was in the kitchen now, still in her dressing gown, making toast for Foxy. Betsy was sitting in her high chair, feeding herself mushy cereal – that is, when her spoon found her mouth; sometimes it found her nose or her hair.

'She ought to wear a fisherman's cape for meals,' said Foxy. 'Then you could just hose her down afterwards.'

Gran came in looking early morning-ish and screwing up her eyes.

'Anyone feen my teef?' she asked. 'And where'f my glaffef? – I need them to find my teef.'

She felt her way to the kitchen table and trod

on Smokey's tail. Smokey squealed and squeezed under the cooker. Foxy's Dad came into the kitchen, which was only small even when it was empty.

'A cup of tea going, is there?' he asked.

Mum turned to put tea bags and boiling water into the teapot. Gran bent down to get Smokey out.

'Come on, come on out, good puss,' she coaxed.

'The toast, Mum, quick,' said Foxy. 'It's burning.'

'Burning, burning – 'ray, 'ray!' cried Betsy. She waved her spoon enthusiastically and a glob of cereal flew across and landed on Smokey, who hissed and shot back under the cooker.

'Now look what you've done,' said Gran.

She straightened up and banged her head on the grill pan, which Mum had just pulled out to blow out the flames on the toast.

'Here's your glasses, Gran,' said Dad.

'Where? Where?' said Gran, rubbing her head with one hand and holding out the other one for the glasses. Dad reached across to give her them and trod in Smokey's saucer of milk. Mum threw the burnt toast in the bin and laid some more slices on the grill pan. Dad hopped round on one foot looking for something to wipe off the milk with. As he did so, another of Betsy's cereal globs landed on his clean foot. It was at this moment that Foxy suddenly remembered.

'Oh, Mum, I've got to take a hard-boiled egg – I've *got* to.'

There was a moment's silence, as all heads turned to look at him.

'A hard-boiled egg?' said his mother faintly. '– Now?'

'It's for a competition,' said Foxy. 'We're going to decorate them for an Easter egg competition.'

'Choccy, choccy, choccy!' shouted Betsy; she knew about Easter eggs.

Dad found a duster and wiped his feet with it.

'Here we are,' said Mum, ferreting about at the back of the fridge. 'It's the last one in the box; it's got a bit of a crack in it.'

'The toast, Mum, it's burning,' cried Foxy again.

''Ray, 'ray!' shouted Betsy excitedly; breakfast wasn't usually this much fun. She raked through her hair with her slimy spoon. Mum blew out more flames.

'This teapot always dribbles,' grumbled Dad, pouring out tea into the mugs and over the table.

Gran picked up the duster to polish her glasses.

'That'f funny, they're all fmeary.'

She screwed up her eyes again and wandered out to look for her teeth. Mum put the egg into boiling water in a saucepan. The water immediately foamed with strings of floating egg white.

'I don't think I'm hungry after all,' said Foxy, as his mother lobbed the third lot of black toast into the bin. He finished off the tea in his mug and started to get his things ready for school.

'Where's my felt-tips, Mum?' he asked.

'Gran had them,' she said. 'She was doing some sort of a competition for Blue Peter with Betsy – where did you put those felt-tips, Betsy?'

'Underpsshed,' said Betsy through a mouthful.

'Oh, no,' groaned Foxy – that meant she'd pushed them into her secret place under the shed and he'd have to grovel in the wet grass trying to reach them.

'I'll have to go without them. Is the egg ready, Mum?'

His mother stared at him.

'The egg? – Oops, the *egg*!'

She dived for the pan which was hissing and spluttering as it boiled dry.

'Well, it's certainly *hard*-boiled,' she said, peering into the brownish pan. She spooned out the cracked, discoloured egg, dropped it into a paper bag and gave it to Foxy.

'Bye, everybody,' he shouted, and hurried off to school.

Not surprisingly, Foxy's egg decoration wasn't very successful. For a start, he hadn't his own felt-tips, so he had to keep begging to borrow other people's. They wanted to use their brightest colours, so he only managed to get brown, black and a sort of sludgy green.

'You could pretend it was a camouflaged egg,' suggested Imran, 'like they have in the army.'

'Why do they want camouflaged eggs in the army?' asked Foxy.

'Well, so the enemy can't see them, I suppose,' said Imran.

Foxy decided against that idea. He set to work to turn his egg into a tortoise. The cracks helped to make the pattern of its shell look quite realistic. He drew its head and four feet and a tiny tail.

'That's really good,' said Imran. 'Really.'

But Foxy knew that Imran's Spiderman egg was much better – and so were several of the others, decorated in clear, bright colours. The Headmaster came in later to judge the eggs. He gave first prize to a really clever face that one of the girls had drawn, second prize to Imran's Spiderman, and third prize to an egg covered in brilliant little butterflies. 'That's great, Immy!' said Foxy, clapping his friend on the back. Everyone except the three winners was secretly disappointed, although Foxy had been pretty sure he wouldn't win; his rather messy design looked more like a stone than a tortoise. The Headmaster stopped on his way out.

'Now don't forget, everyone,' he said. 'Come to the Hall after dinner, for our grand Class Egg-Rolling Competition.'

Foxy had forgotten the egg-rolling; it was quite a tradition. Usually the P.E. benches were lined up, end to end, and rubber mats were placed over them, hanging down to the floor. They provided a slope down which the eggs were rolled. A class at a time knelt behind the benches and let go of their eggs to see which one rolled furthest down the mats and away across the floor of the Hall.

This time four classes went through their heats, and four children excitedly clutched their winning eggs. Then came the turn of Foxy's class. He and Imran and the others knelt down behind the P.E. benches. They each held their egg on the very edge of the bench, so that it had a good long slope to roll down to give it the best start.

'Go!' ordered the Headmaster.

Eggs of all colours hurtled down the slope and sped across the mats. Some trundled to a stop, some went this way and that, bumping into others. A bright red one shot across the floor, followed more slowly by Foxy's tortoise. But then the red one suddenly spun round and came back the way it had gone, leaving the tortoise rolling on until it came to a hesitant stop, furthest from the bench.

'You've won this round!' said Imran, slapping Foxy on the back in his turn.

Foxy grinned and went to collect his prize, a cream egg. He and Imran shared it, a bite at a time, while they waited for the final play-off between all the winning eggs. Foxy found himself right in the middle of the row of competitors. He was afraid that might not be a very favourable position, as the other eggs would probably roll into the middle and stop the tortoise short. He held his egg on the extreme edge of the bench, determined at least to start the race well.

'Go!' said the Headmaster.

The eggs hurtled down the slope. A Humpty-

Dumpty shot ahead, doing fast roly-polies across the floor. A striped egg went sideways, cracking into two others, so that all three came to a stop. A bright blue one seemed to be made of rubber, it was almost bouncing along. The audience was laughing and cheering the eggs on. The tortoise was slowly crawling across the floor behind the rest.

'Oh, go on, go on,' urged Foxy. 'Go *on*, tortoise!'

'Come-on-*tor*-toise,' chanted Foxy's class. 'Come-on-*tor*-toise.'

The Humpty-Dumpty and most of the others had wandered to the sides of the Hall; the tortoise was at least still moving forward, but slowing down.

'Come-on-*tor*-toise,' chanted Mr Tucker's class, louder than ever.

The bouncing blue egg suddenly twizzled round and lurched into the tortoise, sending it forward. Then the blue bouncer stopped. But the tortoise was still lumbering on. They all held their breath until it eventually came to a halt only a metre from the Headmaster's feet.

'The tortoise is the winner!' he declared, laughing and holding it up on high. Rousing cheers from Mr Tucker's class filled the Hall.

'You've done it, you've done it again,' shouted

Imran, pushing him forward. Foxy couldn't
believe his luck as the Headmaster shook his
hand and gave him back the tortoise egg and a
prize. There were more cheers as Foxy grinned
and went back to his classmates. He couldn't
wait to get home and tell everyone his good
news.

'Hello, Foxy,' said Gran, who had found her
teeth. 'Goodness, look at your hands – "What,

will these hands ne'er be clean?'' – they're
covered in paint.'

'No, Gran, that's felt-tip,' he said. 'It got on
there when I was decorating my egg for the
competition.'

Betsy came toddling over to have a look. Then
Foxy told them all about the egg-decorating competition and the tortoise, and how it had managed to win his class heat, and then the Grand
Final of the egg-rolling race.

'Well done,' said Dad.

'What's your prize then?' asked Gran.

'This packet of felt-tips,' said Foxy. 'Isn't it
enormous? Do you see, Betsy? You know what
they're for, don't you?'

Betsy's eyes lit up.

'Underershed,' she beamed.

'And here's the famous tortoise egg,' said
Foxy, pulling it from his pocket. 'You'd never
guess that could beat all the other eggs in the
school, would you?'

He held out the cracked, sludge-coloured egg
on the palm of his hand.

'Mmm,' said Dad. 'It certainly doesn't look like
a champion.'

'It must have been the way I boiled it,' said
Mum.

9

MAY

Cup Final

'Guess what – it's the first Saturday in May next week,' said Dad.

'Oh yes?' said Mum.

'Cup Final Day,' said Dad.

'Oh,' said Mum. 'So I suppose you'll be sitting in a darkened room all day with beer and crisps and the television?'

'Only from eleven onwards,' said Dad. 'That's when they start reporting from Wembley: the weather, the state of the turf, the team members, the ref –'

'All right, all right,' cried Mum. 'The same as last year and the year before that and the year before that – though how you can bear to sit watching from eleven in the morning, when the game itself doesn't start until three, I just don't understand.'

She turned to Foxy.

'And I suppose you'll be glued to the box as well?'

Foxy just grinned at her.

That Saturday Dad was up early. There was a feeling of excitement and expectancy in the air. Gran and Mum were going to town for the day, taking Betsy with them.

'When will you be back?' asked Dad.

'Oh, about six, I expect,' said Mum.

'But you'll miss the whole thing,' he said. 'And the presentation of the Cup and medals and everything.'

'That's the idea,' said Mum and Gran together.

Before they set off on the bus, Mum said:

'Now you don't really mind being left alone all day, do you? You know we're not a scrap interested in football.'

Dad assured them that he didn't mind in the least – in fact, he preferred to be left to enjoy the occasion in peace. He waved them off absent-mindedly, then settled down to arrange everything just as he wanted it. The television set was to face his armchair, with a table at his right hand for refreshments; he also had the double-page sports spread from the paper for handy reference. By ten to eleven he was sitting ready, with his United rosette pinned to his pullover. The curtains were closed and the room was dim except for the television screen. In his imagination he was already standing on the terraces at Wembley.

Foxy wasn't really interested in the build-up to the Final; he only wanted to watch the game itself. He put his head round the door and hissed:

'I'm just going round to Imran's. I'll be back in time for the kick-off.'

'Right – ssshhh,' nodded his Dad. 'See you later.'

The two boys had a good morning together until Imran's Mum called him in for a meal. She said to Foxy:

'Shouldn't you be going for yours now?'

Foxy explained about its being Cup Final day. She tutted sympathetically.

'So you're a football orphan, are you? – poor Foxy. Then you'd better stay and have something with us. It's lucky we're having elastic curry today.'

'Elastic curry?' said Foxy.

'Yes,' she smiled. 'It can always stretch for one more.'

Foxy really enjoyed it; he had been expecting to share a snack with his Dad. But he was still keeping his eye on the time.

'That was great,' he said at half past two. 'But I think I'd better be getting back now.'

'Won't you have another helping of ice-cream?' asked Imran's Mum.

'No, thanks,' said Foxy. 'I must go, Dad's expecting me.'

'Off you go then,' she said. 'I know the kick-off is at three – you'd better not miss that.'

Foxy ran all the way home. He dashed into the house and sat down, panting, his eyes already fixed on the television. The players were lined up in the middle of the Wembley pitch.

'You're just in time,' said Dad. 'The Duke's just going to shake hands with them.'

'Look, he's going to the Rovers first,' said Foxy.

'Don't they look a load of thugs and ruffians?' cried Dad in disgust.

'Now he's going to United.'

'Great lads!' exclaimed Dad. 'Don't they look fighting fit? What a team!'

The ref blew his whistle.

'United have the ball,' cried Foxy.

'Come on now, boys,' said Dad. 'Get stuck in there!'

Both teams went into the attack. The ball thudded this way and that, there were fast passes across the field, and some clever footwork and tackling, as well as some skilful dribbling up the side-lines – but all attempts at goal shots were headed off by the defenders of both teams. To and fro, to and fro, minute after minute after minute. It was very frustrating for everyone, but the teams were evenly matched. When the half-time whistle blew, there was still no score. Dad groaned in despair.

'I don't know if I can stand any more of this,' he said – but he didn't mean it. 'I tell you what, Foxy, just so I don't miss anything, will you do me a favour?'

He dug his hand into his pocket for change.

'Run to the shop and get four more packets of crisps and half a dozen sausage rolls.'

Foxy raced down the road to the shop on the corner. Two other customers were already there. He jigged impatiently from foot to foot while they chatted to the shopkeeper. At last one of the women saw Foxy's face.

'You'd better serve this little'un first,' she said. 'He looks as though he's on pins to get back to the football – am I right?'

Foxy nodded and stammered out:

'F-four packets of c-crisps and six s-sausage rolls, please.'

As the shopkeeper counted out the sausage rolls, he called back over his shoulder to Foxy:

'Salt and vinegar, ready salted, cheese and onion or barbecue beef?'

'Oh, er, the first four you come to,' said Foxy.

The minutes of half-time were ticking away. He bit his lip anxiously.

'Come on, come *on*,' he thought.

The shopkeeper seemed to be working in slow motion. At last, Foxy had the change in his pocket and was cradling the bag of sausage rolls and the packets of crisps in his arms. He made for the shop door. The woman opened it for him with a smile.

'Hope your team wins,' she said.

But Foxy didn't hear. He was thundering down the street and skidding in at the gate. His Dad had left the front door open for him.

'Come on, quick,' called Dad. 'They're just starting again.'

Foxy slumped on to the settee. His heart was pumping wildly and he was prickly with sweat. He tore off his pullover.

'Here,' said Dad, and handed him a glass of lemonade.

'Great,' said Foxy, and drank it straight off.

His Dad refilled the glass and Foxy gulped half of that down, too.

'Can you turn the sound up a bit?' said his Dad.

Foxy put his glass on top of the set while he adjusted the volume.

'Better?' he asked.

'Mmm,' nodded his Dad, his eyes fixed on the screen. 'Here they go again, they've got the ball – come on now, United.'

He leant forward, urging them on.

'Look, Smithy's got the ball now.'

Smithy was United's amazing goal scorer – if anyone could get a goal, it was Smithy.

'Phew, I'm still boiling,' said Foxy, bending down to unlace his trainers.

'Out to the wing – to Jackson!' yelled Dad. 'Now back to Smithy!'

Foxy put one foot behind the other and eased off one of his trainers. His foot was so sweaty that the trainer wouldn't come off. He gave it a sharp jerk to loosen it.

'Run, Smithy! – that man's got two false legs – get a move on, RUN!'

At that moment Foxy's trainer, loosened at last, hurtled through the air and hit the glass of lemonade on top of the television. Smithy was racing towards an opening in Rovers' defence and pulled back his foot to shoot –

But the screen went blank as lemonade poured down inside the set. There was a sudden hissing noise and a cloud of steam rose in the air. There was a burning smell – and the screen stayed blank. Foxy couldn't move a muscle for sheer horror at what he had done.

'FOXY!' yelled his father.

He leapt forward and twiddled all the knobs, but there was no sound and no picture. He unplugged the set at the mains and raced into the kitchen to find the tranny.

'I don't believe this is happening, this can't be true,' he cried. 'Was it a goal or not? – I've got to find out, are they a goal ahead or not?'

The tranny was tuned to Mum's favourite station, not the sports commentary. He twiddled the tuning knob this way and that, but there seemed to be nothing but music.

'I can't find the blessed thing,' he groaned. 'Surely *some*one at the BBC knows the Cup Final's on.'

The tranny needed new batteries, and soon what sound there was, had faded away. Dad looked desperately at his watch.

'It must be nearly all over,' he said wildly. 'I've got to find out what's happening. I know – old Porrett'll be watching – he'll let me see the last few minutes.'

He raced out into the street, shot across the road to Mr Porrett's and banged on the door. Poor Foxy hadn't moved. He was still looking helplessly at the steam fizzing gently from the television. He glanced at his feet – one trainer was still on, the other was lying behind the set next to pieces of broken glass in a pool of lemonade . . .

Soon afterwards, the others returned from town, loaded down with carrier bags, noisy and cheerful. They found the house strangely silent. Foxy and his Dad were both kneeling behind the television set. Foxy was carefully picking up pieces of glass; Dad was trying to dry the carpet and the back of the set with Mum's hair-dryer.

'What on earth are you doing back there?' asked Gran. 'There's no picture at *that* side of the set, you know.'

Dad snarled something that Gran couldn't hear. He was still angry with Mr Porrett for not being in.

'Guess what happened to us,' said Mum brightly. 'We were just walking through the shopping precinct, and there was this crowd of people looking in a shop window. They were

looking into a showroom, watching television. Well, you know we're not normally a bit interested in the Cup Final, but anyway, we stopped and watched for a bit, didn't we, Gran? – and we saw the last few minutes of the match.'

'Yes,' said Gran. 'It was really exciting, wasn't it?'

Dad gritted his teeth; Foxy wished he was ten miles away.

'Wasn't that goal of Smithy's fantastic?' said Mum. 'That man really is magic, isn't he? Still, I don't need to tell you two that: I expect you've been glued to the set ever since we left, haven't you? Did you ever see a goal like it?'

'No,' said Dad and Foxy together. 'No, never.'

10

JUNE

Class Trip

'Are we going on a trip this term, Mr Tucker?' asked Kevin Wilson.

'We usually do in summer, don't we, sir?'

Mr Tucker stroked his beard and looked at his class.

'Any suggestions, then?'

'Go down a coalmine, sir.'

'Go to the theatre.'

'A trip in Concorde.'

'Climb Snowdon.'

'Go round a chocolate factory.'

'Watch the England footy squad training . . .'

Everyone had an idea. Mr Tucker nodded at them all, then said calmly, 'Our coach is already booked for next Friday. You'll be getting letters to take home about it tonight. We're going to the Simbwana Safari Park.'

The following Friday, everyone was in school.

It was the first full attendance for weeks. Mr Farmer, the caretaker, leant on his broom handle and watched them pushing and shoving to get into the coach.

'Don't know why you're paying good money to go to a Safari Park,' he growled to Mr Tucker. 'You can see enough little beasts round here any day.'

'Well, yes, Mr Farmer,' said Mr Tucker. 'But the ones we're going to see are quite wild.'

'That's what I meant,' muttered Mr Farmer.

By now everyone was in the coach. Mr Tucker stood at the front to count heads. 'Twenty-eight, twenty-nine, thirty ... there should be thirty-one – who's missing?'

He opened the register and called all the names. They were all answered. Then he counted heads again – only thirty.

'This is ridiculous; who's missing?' he demanded.

'Perhaps it's me, sir,' came a faint voice from near the back.

'It's Benjy, sir,' said a couple of people nearby. 'You didn't see his head, because he's bending down behind the seat.'

'Sit up, Benjy, for heaven's sake,' exclaimed Mr Tucker. 'What on earth are you doing behind there?'

'Having a nose-bleed, sir,' came the faint voice again.

Mr Tucker raised his eyes to heaven.

'Keep your head back and your nose up,' he ordered.

He passed a wad of paper tissues back to Benjy, and nodded at the driver to get going. The coach soon left town and headed out through green countryside. It was already quite warm. After a while, the driver pulled into a lay-by to open the roof. He rolled up his sleeves and put on dark glasses before starting up again.

'It's going to be a scorcher,' he said.

'I hope it doesn't get too hot,' remarked Lucy, 'or the animals will lie under the trees to keep cool and we'll hardly see them.'

'There was an ace film on telly last night,' said Toothy Beddoes. 'About a place in Africa, where lions and things live – did you see it? There were these lions out hunting, see, and they closed in on a whole load of zebra, and they cut in and separated the straggler that couldn't keep up – a bit like One Man and His Dog, you know: when the sheepdogs get one on its own, then they run after it until it's tired out, and then they pounce on it and eat it.'

'I didn't know sheepdogs ate sheep,' said Lucy.

'No, dum-dum – the lions eat the zebra.'

'Do you think we might see them doing that today?'

'Eugh, no,' squeaked Belinda. 'We've had enough already today, with Benjy and his bleeding nose.'

'What's the matter with my bleeding nose?' demanded Benjy.

'Nothing, nothing at all – just keep your head back and your nose up in the air,' said Lucy hastily.

'But I'm fed up with looking at the ceiling like this,' protested Benjy.

'We'll tell you when there's something good to see outside,' said Shamila.

Conversation died down to a low murmur, interrupted only by a steady rustle of paper bags and chocolate wrappers.

'Can we start our lunch, sir?' asked Shamila.

'Sounds as though most of you are well stuck in already,' commented Mr Tucker. 'Don't forget, that's got to last you until we get home.'

'Don't worry, we've got plenty, sir.'

'Yes, my Mum used a whole loaf on my sarnies.'

'And my Dad gave me a pound to buy crisps and chocolate to bring.'

'Ooh, 'tisn't half hot – wish we had some ice-cubes . . .'

This made everyone feel even hotter and stickier. But now the coach was approaching high wire gates over which hung a notice in enormous letters: Simbwana Safari Park. The children cheered. The coach stopped. Mr Tucker paid the entrance money, and the driver was given instructions at the cash desk. He stood up and shut the roof. Then he put the engine into a low gear and drove in through the gates. Slowly the coach rolled along an unfenced road into open country. A few clumps of trees were dotted here and there on both sides.

'It's just grass and bushes,' said Foxy.

They looked from side to side in disappointment; then Mary-Ann, who was sitting near the front, gave a piercing squeal.

'Look, look – elephants!'

They all shot round in their seats. From behind a distant clump of trees came a group of five elephants. Their ears waved to and fro as they ambled steadily towards the road.

'They're going to come right near us,' squeaked Mary-Ann.

Children at the back stood up and craned forward to see. Several people began to take pictures. The coach crawled forward and the elephants came on steadily.

'We'll run them over,' breathed Sylvia.

'No one can run over elephants,' said Foxy.

The huge creatures stopped in the middle of the road only a few metres ahead and looked at the coach curiously, their trunks swaying as though in greeting. The children held their breath. Then the elephants turned their backs and plodded forward again.

'Ahh,' said everyone. 'That was brill – aren't they ace!'

'I'b habig anudder dose bleed, sir,' called Benjy.

Mr Tucker passed back a second wad of paper hankies.

'It's the excitement,' he said. 'Just keep your head back, Benjy.'

Benjy obediently leant his head back and kept

102

the wodge of tissues over his nose. He fixed his
eyes on the roof of the bus. Suddenly his eyes
widened and he called urgently:

'Bister Tucker, sir, there's bunkeys od the
roof!'

'Can't hear what you're saying, Benjy,' called
back Mr Tucker; but by then everyone else was
gazing up at the window in the roof, where two
furry crouching figures could be seen. Two pairs
of bright eyes stared down in amazement at the
creatures in the coach below. They obviously
thought the sight was a funny one, for they
turned and looked at one another as though in
disbelief, then stared down again, flattening
their noses on the glass. The excitement was too
much for one of them, for a thin trickle of water
began to drip down the outside of one of the
windows.

'They're weeing on the roof!' shrieked
everyone.

'Hey, you young monkeys,' shouted the
driver, who had seen this in his mirror. 'I took
this through the wash this morning – get off my
coach!'

He pressed the windscreen spray button and
started the windscreen wipers at their quickest
speed. Some of the spray shot back over the roof
of the coach and splashed on to the monkeys.

They leapt back in surprise. Then, deciding that they'd seen enough, they swung down and lolloped away sideways over the grass, jabbering at one another and looking as though they were rocking with laughter.

The driver drove on, muttering to himself about his nice clean coach. From the back seats came a sudden click, then – ppsssshshshshshs . . .

'What was that?' asked Mr Tucker, not daring to look round.

'Oh, sir . . . my drink was a bit too fizzy, I think it must have got shaken up . . . could you let me have some tissues to wipe the roof, sir . . .?'

Mr Tucker handed back another wad of paper hankies. Then he lay back in his seat and closed his eyes. The driver drove on, scowling fiercely. They came to some more high gates and entered another compound. Here the trunks of the sparse trees were bare all the way up, except for a crowning topknot of foliage. They soon realized why.

'Look – giraffes, over there!'

Once again they took photographs and craned their necks to see. There were several giraffes, a herd of zebra and some deer.

'What's worse than a giraffe with a sore throat?' asked Tommy Pugh.

'Oh, a centipede with corns – that's an old one.'

In the next compound two Park Rangers drove past them in a Land Rover; they had rifles with them.

'What are they for?' asked Lucy nervously.

'Just for emergencies,' said the driver. 'You'd be surprised at the silly things people do. There was a chap here the other day, got a puncture – and got out to change the wheel, here in the lion compound! There'd have been a heck of a fuss if he'd been mauled . . .'

'What happens if *we* break down, then?' asked Toby.

'We just stay where we are and the Park Ranger patrols will soon spot us and get us towed to a safe place.'

'I'm roasting,' complained Mary-Ann. 'Why can't we open the window?'

'You saw those monkeys,' said the driver. 'They're quite likely to shove an arm through an open window and get you by the hair, or grab the ignition keys and run off with them – no thank *you*!'

The coach rumbled slowly along the dusty road, which was quivering in the heat. Under distant trees groups of lions lay unmoving in the shade.

'Look at that one yawning,' said Imran. 'I bet he's really bored.'

'Why did the Safari Park send for the Telecom man?' asked Tommy Pugh.

'Go on, I'll buy it,' said Mr Tucker with his eyes still closed, 'Why did the Safari Park send for the Telecom man?'

'Because they had a cross lion,' said Tommy.

'I think I'm going to be sick,' wailed Patsy.

'I told you not to bring six strawberry yoghurts,' said Lucy.

'We're nearly back at the main gate,' said Mr Tucker. 'Hang on, Patsy – we'll be getting out in a few minutes at the shopping area.'

Patsy managed to contain herself and the strawberry yoghurts, and soon the coach was turning into a huge car park.

'Be back in one hour prompt,' said Mr Tucker.

The class suddenly found new energy and clattered down the steps in search of postcards, souvenirs and more refreshment. An hour later they wearily hauled themselves back into the coach. Mr Tucker stood up to count heads before the journey home.

'Twenty-nine, thirty . . . that's funny, there should be thirty-one . . . oh no, where's Benjy?'

'Here, sir,' came a faint voice from behind a seat.

Mr Tucker heaved an exasperated sigh.

'I suppose it's your bleeding nose again, Benjy?'

'No, sir,' said Benjy. 'It's my bleeding knee. It's dripping on to my trainers. I was running to get in the ice-cream queue and I fell over.'

Without a word, Mr Tucker passed back a wad of tissues. He looked flushed and hot; his sleeves were rolled up and his shirt was open at the neck. He was fanning himself with the class register. He wearily nodded at the driver to start up. Some of the children hung over the back of his seat to show him what they had bought.

'Do you like my animal postcards, sir? They're for my safari diary.'

'And I got a lion pencil sharpener – you stick the pencil in its mouth, see?'

'Look at my stick of rock: it says Simbwana all the way through – would you like a bite, sir?'

'No thanks, Tommy,' said Mr Tucker. 'I don't really feel very hungry.'

'Look here – see what I got: it's a car sticker with lots of animals on,' said Foxy. 'We thought we could put it on the classroom window.'

'Oh yes?' said Mr Tucker.

'And look here,' said Imran. 'Under the picture it says, "We've been for a great day out at the Simbwana Safari Park."'

'Yes,' said Foxy. 'Well, we have, haven't we, sir?'

Mr Tucker smiled.

'I'm glad you think so, Foxy,' he said. 'Really glad.'

11

JULY

Summer Fair

It was Friday and a school morning. But there wasn't the usual Thank-goodness-it's-the-end-of-the-week feeling, because next day the school's Summer Fair was to be held. Children were crossing the playground carrying cake tins or hauling bulging carrier bags. Mr Tucker stood in the main doorway like a policeman directing traffic.

'Cakes and groceries down to Class 1 . . . bottles for the bottle stall into the Hall . . . jumble to Class 3 . . . toys and books along to Mrs Cress-well's class . . .'

Mr Tucker's own class was going to be looking after the plant stall. The window-sills were already crammed with pots of cacti and spider plants, and round the walls were standing buckets of mint and cut flowers.

'Well, it doesn't look as though we'll be getting much work done today,' said Mr Tucker, when he came in. Everyone brightened up.

'So we've been given the job of poster-making. I've plenty of paper and large felt-tips. I want you to work in pairs. Make the lettering large, so it's easy to read from a distance. We want posters for the plant stall, the pony rides, the balloons, the ice-creams, Simon the Snorkel –'

'Ooh, what's that, sir?'

'That's what they're bringing from the fire station,' said Mr Tucker. 'It's an enormous fire engine with a hydraulic platform: the ladder goes up about thirty metres into the air, and there's a safety platform at the top of the ladder –'

'Oh, yes, I know, sir,' said Foxy. 'And the men can stand on there and get close up to burning buildings and things with the hosepipes.'

'That's right,' nodded Mr Tucker. 'And tomorrow the firemen will have their uniforms and fire-fighting equipment and so on, on show. It should be most interesting – but for the moment, I still need volunteers to make posters for jumble, fancy goods and sweets . . .'

Next day was dry.

'That's good,' said Foxy. 'That means we can have all the stalls in the playground. You're coming, aren't you, Mum?'

'Wouldn't miss it,' said Mum, 'and Betsy's been looking forward to the pony rides for ages.'

'Gee up – gallopy, gallop!' shouted Betsy, kicking her heels into her high-chair.

'Are you coming, Dad?' asked Foxy.

'Well, Summer Fairs aren't really my scene,' said Dad, lowering the newspaper, 'and there's so much to do in the garden –' he made a rueful face. 'You know what it's like for us gardeners at this time of year: mowing the grass, weeding, clipping the hedge –'

'Oh, all right, you needn't come then,' said Foxy. 'But will you give me something to spend for you?'

His father muttered a little, but dug in his pocket and pulled out a handful of change. He gave Foxy some silver.

'Ah, great,' said Foxy. 'Thanks, Dad.'

'Are you lot ever coming?' asked Gran.

She loved jumble sales and Summer Fairs, and wanted to get there in good time for the bargains. She helped Betsy get ready, then she took her hand and the four of them set off down the street. Several other families were on their way to school too, some of them carrying last-minute jumble, or cakes and samosas still warm from the oven.

'There's Imran,' said Mum.

Imran was shouting something at them and pointing behind them. They turned round.

Smokey was following them down the street.

'I thought I shut her in,' said Mum. 'Dad must have let her out.'

Foxy yanked Smokey up in his arms, ran back to the garden with her and plonked her down inside the gate. Then he ran back to catch up the others.

They could already hear music blaring from down the street. Strings of balloons hung from the school fence, and above the gate was stretched a length of computer paper on which Mr Tucker's class had written in bright colours: WELCOME TO OUR SUMMER FAIR.

'See you back home later, Foxy,' said Mum, and disappeared with Gran and Betsy into the crowd. The playground was already busy with people dawdling from stall to stall. Over on the grass was a group of girls with the ponies. But the centre of attraction was parked in the far corner near the oak tree.

There stood Simon the Snorkel, gleaming red and silver, long and powerful. The hydraulic ladder was folded back flat along the roof. Several uniformed firemen stood alongside Simon.

'Wow,' said Foxy.

He and Imran stared for a minute, then he said:

'Let's look at everything else first, and save that for last.'

They spent half an hour looking at all the stalls and watching the display of morris dancing. They took their turn at working behind the class plant stall. Then they stood next to Mr Tucker and his shove-a-copper game.

'Roll up, roll up, come and shove a copper,' he shouted. 'And when I say shove a copper, I don't mean push a policeman over – I mean shove your spare coppers along the board and win double your money if you don't touch a line . . . All in a good cause, roll up, ladies, gentlemen and children, bring your coppers here . . .'

After this the two boys bought ice-creams and rolls of comics, then they stood in the sunshine and shared a bowl of strawberries and cream. Suddenly Imran waved his spoon wildly.

'Hey, look, there's your Smokey, do you see? Just disappearing behind that stall, look, there's her fluffy tail.'

'Stupid animal,' grumbled Foxy. 'She's always following me. She hasn't the sense she was born with. Look, now she's shot behind another stall – we'll never catch her.'

'Now she's slinking round the edge of the grass – oh, no!'

Someone had trodden on Smokey's tail and

she suddenly shot out in front of the hooves of the leading pony – on which Betsy was sitting. The pony was startled and lifted its forelegs. The girl leading it was taken by surprise and let the reins go slack. It jerked away and began to trot smartly across the grass. Betsy was joggled down on to her tummy, and lay there, along the saddle, shouting gleefully, 'Gallopy, gallop – gallopy, gallop!'

Foxy dropped his spoon and raced across the grass. He managed to haul his sister off into his arms as the pony went past.

'More, more,' shouted Betsy, straining away from Foxy to get back on the pony.

'Certainly not, no more,' cried Mum, coming up breathlessly and grabbing Betsy in her arms. 'I think that's quite enough gallopy-gallop for one day.'

Foxy grinned and went back to his friend.

'Oh, you rotten thing, you've finished the strawbs.'

'Course I did,' said Imran. 'You went off and left them – come on, let's go over to the fire engine now.'

They were allowed to look all over it, even stand at the controls. The firemen let them each try on a yellow safety helmet. The ladder was partly extended, with its platform in the air. The boys looked up at it, as the Chief Fireman showed them how it could be made to fold slowly down flat again. Suddenly a movement in the oak tree beyond the hydraulic platform caught Imran's eye.

'It's your moggy again,' he said to Foxy. 'She's up in the tree now – look, right up there.'

'Stupid creature,' exclaimed Foxy. 'I told you she hadn't the sense she was born with. The pony must have frightened her – we'll never get her down now.'

'Do you want to get her down?' asked the fireman, who had been listening.

'Yes, of course,' said Foxy. 'She got up in a tree once before and was too frightened to come down. We had to get the window cleaner to bring his ladder.'

'Well, you don't need the window cleaner this time,' said the fireman. 'We'll use the hydraulic platform. It'll be a good practice exercise for us.'

He had a few words with one of his mates. Then he helped the two boys on to the platform at the front of the ladder. There was a rail all round which they gripped tightly, wondering what was going to happen. There was a loud humming sound, and very slowly, v-e-r-y s-l-o-w-l-y, the hydraulic platform began to rise into the air. Soon it was level with the foliage of the oak tree. Foxy's knuckles were white with gripping the rail; he didn't dare leave go – he'd never been so high off the ground before.

'Oh, look at that stupid cat,' he cried. 'She's climbing up even further.'

'But she's moving nearer to us along that branch,' said Imran.

The platform rose a little higher. The fireman leant over the branch where Smokey was balancing, but Smokey didn't know him, and tried to retreat a few steps. She missed her footing, but managed to cling on with three paws. She was looking very frightened now.

'I think it's up to you, sonny,' said the fireman.

He helped Foxy to edge further along the platform, so that he was the nearest to Smokey. The platform swung a little further into the leaves. Foxy swallowed hard. He didn't want to leave go of the rail – but he could see poor Smokey's big scared eyes among the leaves . . .

'Come on then, Smoke,' he said, trying to speak soothingly. 'There's n-nothing to b-be scared about. Come to Foxy then, and we'll s-soon have you safely down again. Come on, there's a good girl – got you! – now hold tight to Foxy.'

He had managed to lift her claws free of the branch, and now he had her tight in his arms.

She had sunk her claws into his neck, but he didn't even notice.

'Well done, lad,' said the fireman briskly. 'Now let's be going down.'

Foxy drew a deep breath, still holding Smokey as tightly as he could. Imran leaned over and rubbed the top of her head. The platform was swinging out from the tree and slowly descending.

For the first time the boys' legs stopped trembling and they felt able to look at the view.

'It's like being in space,' said Imran. 'There's nothing under us at all.'

This made Foxy feel nervous again, as he hadn't a free hand to grip the rail with. The fireman put a steadying hand on his shoulder – that felt better.

'We're as high up as the birds,' he forced himself to say. 'Look over there, that's the park with the paddling pool – and look, there's our street.'

'Oh yes,' said Imran, 'and there's the shop on the corner – and there's the green roof of your shed – see? What's that white thing next to your shed?'

Foxy narrowed his eyes in the sunlight, concentrating on the tiny speck of white in his back garden.

'It's somebody – I think it must be Dad, with a white thing on his head. I bet he's sitting in a deckchair, and I bet that's a hanky on his head. He always does that when it's hot – ties knots in his hanky and puts it on his head. He says it stops the flies from skidding on his bald patch.'

The platform was nearly back down on a level with the school roof. Smokey was purring loudly, pushing her claws into Foxy's neck in time with her purrs. It felt like little pins going in and out.

'I think she'll be OK now,' said Foxy. 'I'll take her straight home.'

The boys thanked the fireman several times as he helped them scramble down to the ground. Their legs were suddenly very weak and wobbly. But they were glad to be standing on the safe old playground again. They were surprised to be met by a crowd of their classmates.

'That was a great rescue,' breathed Lucy.

'Oh, thanks,' said Foxy with a casual smile. 'It was nothing really.'

'What was it like up there? What was it like?' asked everyone, pushing to get near them.

Foxy put on a drawling Star Trek accent.

'We were conquering space – the final frontier . . .' he said, but his legs still felt like jelly.

Still clutching Smokey, he pushed his way

behind Imran to the school gate. They went straight to Foxy's and left Smokey shut in the kitchen. Then Gran, Mum and Betsy arrived. They slumped down exhausted, surrounded by cakes, plants and balloons. Betsy stuck out a bright red tongue to show them she'd had two ice-lollies.

'*And* a whole bag of jalebis,' she boasted.

'Well, you look as though you've all had a good time,' said Dad, coming in from the garden.

'What about you, dear?' asked Mum. 'Have you had a good afternoon? I hope you've not been overtiring yourself.'

'Well, you know what it's like for us gardeners at this time of year,' said Dad. 'We don't seem to have time to draw breath, what with the mowing, the weeding, the hedge-clipping, the –'

' – Sitting in a deckchair,' said Foxy.

'Me? Sit in a deckchair?' exclaimed Dad. 'I've hardly stopped . . .' Imran and Foxy grinned at him.

'Show us your hanky then,' said Foxy.

Dad looked puzzled and pulled out his hanky. Each corner had a large knot tied in it. Everyone looked at it and burst out laughing.

'You *have* been sitting in the sun,' said Gran.

'Well, perhaps for two seconds – just to get my

breath back . . . Anyway, who told you? Who let the cat out of the bag?'

Imran and Foxy grinned at one another.

'Well,' said Foxy. 'I suppose Smokey did.'

12

AUGUST

Holiday

Foxy and Imran strolled along the High Street, licking ice-creams.

'It's melting too quickly out here in the sun,' said Foxy. 'Let's go into Woollies – it'll be cooler in there.'

They sauntered round the store, just enjoying doing nothing in particular.

'There's those little tins of enamel paint I need to paint my Airfix model with,' said Foxy. 'But I've no money left anyway.'

Imran fished in his pocket and brought out a pound coin. 'That's all I've got,' he said, 'but you can borrow it, if you like.'

He held it out to Foxy on the palm of his hand. Smack! Imran's hand shot upward, the coin flew in the air and was swiftly caught.

'*I'll* have that,' said a voice behind the boys.

A large youth in a black leather jacket stood there, a look of triumph on his pasty face.

'Gimby!' exclaimed Foxy in dismay. Gimby had left their school only a couple of years before, and was well known and disliked in the neighbourhood. He had always been a sworn enemy of Mr Farmer, the school caretaker, and he was seldom seen without his equally unpleasant companion, Bas Nutter. Someone strolled round the paint stand and stood next to Gimby.

'Oh . . . er . . . Nutter,' gulped Foxy. 'I didn't see you were there too.'

'Yeah, well I am, and me and Gimby need that money more than you two little squirts – we're having a bit of a cash-flow crisis, eh, Gimby? Heh, heh . . .'

'That's stealing,' scowled Foxy.

'Eh? What? Didn't quite catch that,' said Gimby, treading carefully on both of Foxy's feet, so he couldn't get away. Nutter, meanwhile, was standing so close to them that Imran could see the spots on his neck above his denim jacket. Nutter smiled nastily at Imran.

'Did you have something to say, too?' he invited softly. 'Come on – free country.'

Imran shook his head and looked down at the floor. He just wanted them to go away. A shop assistant walked past. Foxy looked at her and tried to signal his desperation with his eyes, but he knew it was hopeless.

'Come on, Nutter,' said Gimby. 'We've got enough for what we need – now these nice little boys have offered to help us.'

He aimed a vicious kick at Foxy, but Foxy had been expecting something of the sort, and somehow leapt sideways and avoided it. He and Imran walked away as fast as they could from the paint stand, and didn't stop until they were safe among the shoppers at the other side of the store. Then they dared to look back. Nutter and Gimby were queuing up at the cash desk to pay for cans of spray paint.

'We ought to tell someone,' said Foxy indignantly.

'They wouldn't believe us,' said Imran. 'It's only our word against theirs.'

'But we can't let them get away with that,' said Foxy. 'It's so unfair – great bullies . . .'

'Yobs,' said Imran.

'Thick as two short planks,' said Foxy.

They looked at each other, shrugged and wandered outside again.

'It's just not fair,' they kept repeating. 'Just not fair . . .'

They walked down the High Street, then turned into School Road almost automatically, as they did every morning of term. They mooched along the grassy verge at the edge of the road, scuffing up the dust. Patches of melted tar sparkled in the sunlight. They felt sticky with the heat – especially after their brush with Nutter and Gimby.

'Haven't you any money left at all?' asked Imran. 'We could've gone swimming.'

Foxy pulled out the linings of both his trouser pockets: nothing.

'All right, all right, so swimming is out – OK.'

A large pyramid of gravel, dumped by the Highways Department, barred their way along the grass verge. They climbed up it and sat on top.

'Hang on a mo,' said Imran, 'I've got something in my shoe.'

Foxy was too hot to answer. He sieved the cool gravel through his fingers. The road ahead was sending up quivering waves of heat, as though from a pool of water. He pointed it out to Imran.

'Look, that's a mirage,' he said. 'Like travellers see in the desert. Then when they get there it's not water at all, it's a sort of trick of the light – then it disappears.'

'I wish Nutter and Gimby had been a trick of the light,' said Imran. 'I'd be glad never to see them again.'

'Where do you think they've gone?' asked Foxy.

'Probably using that paint to re-spray some old motorbike,' said Imran.

'Or even a stolen car,' said Foxy. 'Wouldn't put it past them.'

Imran looked horrified.

'We should have told someone,' he said. 'I told you we should.'

'That's not true – *I* told *you* we should.'

'Rubbish!'

Foxy gave Imran a push in the chest, so he fell over backwards, clutching at Foxy's ankle as he fell. They both rolled down the gravel slope and fell in a dusty sprawling heap. Suddenly Foxy grabbed his friend by the shirt and pulled him down into the ditch behind the gravel.

'Ssshh,' he hissed. 'Here they come.'

'Who?'

'Nutter and Gimby, of course ... We can watch where they go and follow.'

'See if they are going to re-spray a stolen car.'

'How would we know it was stolen?'

'Well, we could memorize the number in case the police made inquiries.'

'Ssshh, here they come – quick, duck!'

In spite of the heat, Gimby's face looked whiter than ever above his black jacket. Nutter was tall and very thin; his jeans and jacket both looked as though they were several sizes too

127

tight. They trudged along without speaking, but Foxy and Imran could hear them panting in the hot sunshine. Hardly daring to breathe, they peered round the side of the gravel.

Gimby aimed his can of spray at a passing butterfly, but it fluttered away unharmed. They crossed the road to an old cottage which had a To Let sign by the gate. Nutter sprayed his paint on to the notice and they stood back and cackled gleefully.

'Toilet,' whooped Gimby and smacked Nutter on the back.

They carried on down the road, then pushed their way through a gap in the hedge bordering the school field.

'What've they gone in there for?' wondered Foxy, straightening up. 'There's no cars in the school grounds.'

'There's nothing in there at all in the holidays,' said Imran, 'except old Farmer. Come on, we've still got to follow them.'

They crossed the road, went through the same gap in the hedge and hid behind the bushes at the side of the school. Everything was very quiet. Nutter and Gimby were walking openly past the classroom windows, and were now standing facing the long blank wall on the side of the Hall. They must have thought they had the place to themselves, for they pulled out their cans of paint. Nutter started painting red squiggles, but Gimby began to write in large green letters. Gradually Foxy and Imran made out:

FATTY FARMER IS A . . .

'They think old Farmer's away,' said Foxy, 'but I know he's staying at home this holiday, he was telling us.'

Imran was still staring at what Gimby was writing.

'Ooh, hoo, old Farmer won't like that – not one bit,' he said.

'We've got to do something,' hissed Foxy. 'What shall we do? Shall we tell him – before they do worse damage, like break in or something?'

'No, he'll think we've got something to do with it, you know what he's like – besides, I suppose he might just be out.'

'Mmmm,' Foxy frowned thoughtfully, jigging his hands up and down in his pockets. He glanced down and his face suddenly brightened. 'Hey, look, Immy – gravel chippings – I must have put them in my pocket without realizing it. Watch this –'

He took a tiny pebble and threw it as hard as he could at the caretaker's house on their left. It hit the door with a sharp click. He threw another, then another, and more. Imran took a few and threw them too. Soon gravel was bouncing like hailstones against Mr Farmer's door.

It suddenly swung open and he looked out fiercely. The two boys crouched down behind the bushes, their hearts pounding. Mr Farmer was a very big man indeed; he could carry the school dustbins one-handed, and was able to tear telephone directories in half – just as he often threatened to tear evil-doers limb from limb . . .

Now he was looking down at the gravel which had landed on his front step. They could see him frowning and trying to work it out. Then, surprisingly, instead of letting rip with his usual thunderous roar of rage, he was looking round cunningly. They watched him step out on the balls of his feet, making his way silently round the school walls. Imran and Foxy held their breath. Round to their right, they could see that Nutter had now also taken to writing; in red letters he had already sprayed:

'This school is a loony bin, and old Farmer is the biggest loo – '

At this point he was hauled off his feet by old Farmer himself. In a moment he was dangling by his collar from the caretaker's mighty fist. In

three silent strides, old Farmer appeared behind
Gimby and had lifted him off the ground in the
same way. He shook them both and they jerked
limply, too shocked to speak.

They were carried forcibly to the Farmer's
Den, and appeared inside. Several minutes later
they reappeared with steaming buckets and a
scrubbing brush each. The caretaker himself was
hard on their heels, shouting at them to look
lively.

'You young vandals, you yobs, move your
slovenly selves before I help you move them –

and get rid of every speck of paint off these walls before nightfall, or else . . .'

'When's nightfall?' whispered Imran.

'Oh – about half past nine tonight,' said Foxy. 'It took me ages getting that writing of yours off Mrs Reed's wall at Hallowe'en, and that was only chalk.'

They shook hands vigorously, grinning, then crept back to the gap in the hedge. They strolled slowly back towards the town. A motorbike could be heard approaching behind them. It seemed to be slowing down, so they turned.

'Hi,' said Foxy. 'It's Mr Tucker.'

'Thought I recognized you two,' he said, sitting back and pushing up his goggles. 'I've just been into school to collect something. Mr Farmer was on the warpath: he's just discovered a couple of yobbos with spray paint. I wouldn't like to be in their shoes. Well, how are you two enjoying the holidays?'

'OK,' shrugged Foxy. 'Bit boring really.'

'Yes,' said Imran. 'There's more to do at school.'

'Well, once you get back, you'll be so busy, your feet won't touch the ground – you'll be in Miss Clark's class.'

Mr Tucker switched on the engine. It stuttered noisily and blew out a cloud of blue exhaust.

'It won't be as good as this year's been,' said Foxy.

'Course it will,' said Mr Tucker. 'You'll see, it'll be just as good – only different.'

He adjusted his goggles and gave the boys a quick wave. Foxy and Imran stood and watched the motorbike until it was out of sight.

'Right,' said Imran. 'Let's think what to do now, Foxy.'